Cheryl,

May God Bless
You All the Days
of your Life.

Sis. Dawn M.

The
ASSIGNED RISK

A Dreamseer Novel

Dawn E. Collins

WESTBOW
P R E S S
A DIVISION OF THOMAS NELSON

WestBow Press books may be ordered through booksellers or by contacting:

WestBow Press
A Division of Thomas Nelson
1663 Liberty Drive
Bloomington, IN 47403
www.westbowpress.com
1-(866) 928-1240

ISBN: 978-1-4497-5505-8 (sc)
ISBN: 978-1-4497-5504-1 (hc)
ISBN: 978-1-4497-5506-5 (e)

Library of Congress Control Number: 2012910608

Printed in the United States of America

WestBow Press rev. date: 6/28/2012

DEDICATION

THIS WORK IS DEDICATED to the love of Jesus Christ, for He has given me life. To my dearly beloved mother who has gone on home—Anna Roberta Collins—I miss you more than I could have ever imagined possible. We'll meet again. To my son Ian, whose love and support I deeply cherish—God has given me a wonderful gift in you. You've never disappointed me. I love you.

ACKNOWLEDGEMENTS

I'D LIKE TO THANK all of my brothers and sisters; Vince, Debbie, Roberta, Kevin, Billy and Candy for their love and support. It's been difficult without Mom—but we're gonna be just fine. A very special shout out to my brother Carvel, who calls me practically every morning just to check up on me—so faithful. To my longtime friend and confidant, Denise Beckett—thank you for more than twenty years of just being you. To Stephanie Smith—you have shown me a new level of friendship. You're amazing! A special thanks to Cathy Beans, whose friendship defies explanation. We are truly soul-sisters. Or, as I like to put it—sisters from another 'other'. And to those of you, too many to name, who called, sent a text, hit me up on Facebook, or simply prayed for me; thank you, thank you, thank you. I love you all.

For God does speak—now one way, now another—though man may not perceive it. In a dream, in a vision of the night, when deep sleep falls on men as they slumber in their beds, he may speak in their ears and terrify them with warnings, to turn man from wrongdoing and keep him from pride, to preserve his soul from the pit, his life from perishing by the sword.
—*Job 33:14–18 (NIV)*

Deep into that darkness peering, long I stood there, wondering, fearing, doubting, dreaming dreams no mortal ever dared to dream before.
—*Edgar Allan Poe*

PROLOGUE

And he dreamed, and behold a ladder set up on the
earth, and the top of it reached to heaven: and behold
the angels of God ascending and descending on it.
—Genesis 28:12 (KJV)

HE PIERCED THROUGH THE roof of the ivy-thatched colonial home unobserved by mere mortals. Vibrant colors flashed like lightning from his garment with every calculated advance. Intricately tiered wings adorned his fiery, bronzed figure—four wings in total. Two afforded movement between the earth and the second heavens, where the battles waged. Two served as an impenetrable armor. Fully extended, the contoured appendixes spanned the breadth of the subject's house.

Lariel's stature bore the markings of a distinguished warrior. His towering, majestic frame cast a striking silhouette as he descended upon the bedroom. The guardian surveyed the remainder of the house without leaving his station. His eyes burned with unwavering purpose. Nothing escaped his view, for the walls were as glass.

Outside, the darkened, deep blue skies tingled in weighty anticipation. Peculiar shadows sifted through the night, distorting the natural rhythm of the clouds. Everything was in place. The stage had been set.

Hovering above his unsuspecting subject, Lariel positioned himself beneath the vaulted ceiling, creating an impregnable canopy over the four-post bed below. There would be no interference. His cherubic brilliance gradually faded as he settled in for the evening.

He sensed an atmospheric shift in the room. The guardian had a visitor.

"My prince." Lariel bowed before his commander, Michael, whose presence exuded formidable authority.

"You've been briefed on the urgency of this mission." It was not a question.

"Yes," Lariel reported. "Gabriel has reviewed the matter with me."

"We're picking up an unusual amount of activity in the heavens." Disdain flittered across Michael's face. "The enemy has learned of this chosen one's assignment. His minions are posted nearby."

"I have canvassed the premises. The house is secure."

"Excellent. You will guard your subject throughout the night and resist every threat of intrusion. There is no room for error. Everything must go according to plan."

"Understood," Lariel assured his superior. "I will keep them at bay. Do you anticipate direct confrontation?"

"Possibly. Although I suspect the Deceiver is merely placing his feelers out there for now. He will not engage until he believes he has obtained full disclosure. But if he does strike, you must not withstand him entirely—only to the extent necessary," Michael instructed.

"My prince?"

"The subject must engage. The Highest has given the order."

"He will not be disappointed."

"For the Highest and for the Lamb!"

"For the Highest and for the Lamb!" Lariel echoed, bowing as the prince departed, leaving a violent trail of radiance.

Lariel extended his wings to full battle position. He had discerned the peripheral presence of enemy forces maintaining their safe distance. The contingent was well acquainted with the guardian. Their unveiled contempt electrified the air, but they would come no further. Prince Michael's unannounced appearance had undoubtedly caused a flurry of activity. A dispatcher was most certainly on his way back to their headquarters to deliver the news. The Deceiver would not be pleased.

Lariel considered his mission. He had been appointed to this human before she was conceived. Lower ranking officers kept him abreast of her status. Every movement had been monitored with the meticulous accuracy of a master surgeon. However, this was a special assignment. Lariel's presence was specifically ordered, and the instructions were clear. He was not to leave his post for any reason. The prince alone had the authority to relieve him.

Such undertakings generally required special forces, but a series of conquests over the last century had changed that. Lariel was capable of overseeing this operation without immediate reinforcement. Gabriel would dispatch additional troops to provide assistance if need be.

The guardian had learned from past confrontations that the tactics of the adversary were never to be underestimated. He had the battle scars to prove it. His status had been hard won, yet he understood only too well the eternal penalty for pride and arrogance. He would not let his guard down again.

Lariel turned his full attention to the task at hand. His sword was drawn.

He said to them, I have had a dream that troubles me and I want to know what it means.
—Daniel 2:3 (NIV)

CHAPTER I

THE SUBJECT STIRRED BENEATH crumpled sheets, unaware of the celestial activity infiltrating her home. She lingered in the shadows of her subconscious, struggling to wake up. But she could not. Suspended between dream and reality, Samara Daniels wrestled with her destiny. She sensed the presence of a curious element, even in her precarious state. It hinted at the existence of something near yet, at the same time, far off. Wearied, she curled in a fetal position, reluctantly surrendering to the dream.

She was late—even in her dreams. Samara thrust the titanium blue, five-speed, Mustang GT convertible in reverse. Her rear bumper scraped the curb as the car cleared the sidewalk. Backing out of the driveway, she turned onto the tree-lined street and careened toward town, driving faster than normal. Normal for her, that is. Her friends called her "Ms. Daisy" because she typically drove just under the speed limit, no matter what it was. But this time she was driving more recklessly than she cared to admit. She was actually *doing* the speed limit.

Her ex-husband, Anthony Daniels Sr., had texted her on her Blackberry.

"Meet me for dinner?"

She read the text again.

"Please come. It's important."

Samara's stomach lurched and churned as she shifted to third. She reckoned it either butterflies or nausea. Whichever way the pendulum swung, she was far too anxious. The very idea of seeing Tony face-to-face resurrected feelings she thought were pronounced dead and properly buried. He had deserted her and the kids nearly three years ago and had not been heard from since the divorce. Samara had come home from work to find all traces of his things gone. Without notice. Without discussion. Without his family. He was simply, and painfully, gone. And suddenly she gets this mysterious text message.

Samara checked the digital clock on the dashboard again.

"Let him wait." She said, as she reached for the Pepto tablets nestled in her center console. "See how it feels."

Tony had asked to meet at a sports bar located on the corner of Delancey and South. It was just like him to set up a meeting in a crowded, noisy place. She clenched the steering wheel with a death grip so tight that it would take the Jaws of Life to wrench it loose. The bar scene did not suit her at all. Dark places made her nervous. But if Tony was reaching out, he needed help. Not that he deserved it, but he was the father of their children, after all.

She pulled onto Delancey, shifted to neutral, and killed the engine.

"What am I doing?" She plopped her ponytailed head against the headrest. "Repeat after me: I do *not* want him back."

Samara digested her surroundings. Summer had beckoned the neighbors outdoors. Giggling little girls jumped double-dutch in rhythmic splendor on the asphalt sidewalk. Their intricately woven braids bounced gracefully with every skilled maneuver between the ropes. Samara smiled at the thought of joining them.

Local teens gathered around a makeshift basketball court, choosing sides and predicting impending conquests. The contest was mostly about who could out-talk whom. Carefree laughter floated through the summer breeze. Discarded sneakers dangled from phone lines high above the friendly mayhem, indifferent to the relentless clamor. It was a typical midsummer evening in the city.

The wafting aroma of the sports bar's famous Philly cheese steaks seeped through the car window. Samara had not eaten all day. Her stomach growled on cue in angry confirmation. She glanced in her rearview for a final makeup check. Satisfied, she stepped out of the car and onto the busy street in her favorite pair of Steve Maddens. Special times called for special shoes. The four-inch pumps accented the dress that hugged her in all the right places. If she was going to meet the man, then she was going in style.

Oh well, girl, handle your business.

The streetlamp bore down on their prearranged meeting place like an iridescent spotlight. Teetering in her new heels, Samara approached the establishment that had been a staple in the city of Philadelphia for nearly a quarter of a century. The closer she got, the more she had a mind to turn around and go home, as if she had *some* couth. But she was drawn to the bar like a hog to squalor. She couldn't turn back now, even if she wanted to—which she didn't. Besides, she had worn the shoes. And the dress.

Too late to wimp out. You're here now.

Samara cupped her hands and examined the scene through the oval-shaped window etched in the center of the ornately carved wood door. She spotted Tony leaning against the bar. He appeared to be involved in a heated discussion. The muscle-toned arms peeking out from his short-sleeved Polo shirt confirmed his membership at the gym was still active. She watched as he reached across the bar to grab a handful of peanuts. Those arms had comforted her on many occasions. Her heart raced.

"Get a grip," she reprimanded herself. "This is business, nothing personal."

She had mustered the courage to go inside when a peculiar sight caught her attention. A mysterious robed figure had appeared out of thin air and was hovering curiously close to Tony. It literally came from nowhere. Samara squinted, peering closer.

The bar was fairly well lit, yet the hooded apparition concealed itself in the thick darkness of its own existence. If you did not otherwise perceive its presence, you did not see it. Samara saw it. Layers of bottomless shadows shrouded its form. The bowed head belied its posture. Its veiled appearance suggested masculinity. However, it wasn't human.

"What is *that*?" She whispered.

Samara stepped inside the bar, immediately drawing back. A foul stench assaulted her nostrils. The ominous being secreted a putrid odor that saturated every bit of free air. It reeked of old garbage left to bake in the boiling summer sun. The stagnant air draped her body like a wet, woolen blanket. Samara swallowed hard, inhaling the stifling hostility. A horrifying premonition coiled up her spine, chilling her insides.

The creature was expecting her. She wasn't sure how she knew, but she knew. All other activity swirled around them as if everyone else were operating in another dimension of space and time. It seemed that only Samara and the dark angel existed in the invisible vortex. Her brain screamed, *Run!* but her feet refused to obey, as if a greater force were in charge.

"He's mine." The faceless creature spoke without lifting its head.

There was no audible voice, yet Samara heard the statement clearly, as though she were reading its mind. The evil presence communicated telepathically and knew Samara heard. It still had not moved from its place behind Tony.

"He's mine and he doesn't know it," the demon snarled.

Without warning, a sensation of scorching hot arrows pierced Samara's body in rapid sequence. She stumbled backwards, dazed and confused. The demon had no weapons that she could see, yet she felt excruciating pain exploding in her stomach. It was as if the telepathic messages were her attacker's ammunition. Each projected thought penetrated her body like a perfectly aimed javelin.

Samara grabbed her stomach, praying that someone would see. But no one else seemed to be aware of the parallel existence. She was trapped in the unseen hemisphere.

"Tony!" she screamed for her ex-husband.

Tony was standing only a few feet away but was oblivious to the confrontation.

"You're too late." The demon was relentless. "He's given up."

On instinct, Samara raised her arms to shield her body from the next strike. It didn't help. The menacing shadow discharged another torrent of stinging projectiles. Flaming darts exploded in the upper part of her body, knocking her to her knees. She felt exposed and ill equipped to deal with such a formidable opponent.

"Tony, help me!" She tried once more to reach her ex-husband.

"You're wasting your time." The demon mocked her. "He's in no position to discern me, or you."

"That's not true." Samara barely whispered.

"His soul has been delivered to me."

"I don't believe you."

Burning needles scratched at her insides like jagged bits of searing metal. Samara hunched over, drawing her body in. She did not know how to defend herself. The pain was almost unbearable and clogged her ability to reason. If she couldn't get Tony's attention, she would have to figure a plan of escape by herself.

"God help me!" Samara's trembling voice was foreign to her own ears.

"There is no God." The dark spirit challenged her faith at the very core. "Don't believe everything you read."

"If there's no God, why are you here?" She pressed her assailant. "Who are you?"

The demon did not intend to provide any insight. Fallacy and confusion were its secret weapons. It was tapping in to that place where Samara often questioned the validity of her faith. Her gnawing doubts and passive approach to her Christian walk had provided access for this evil darkness. She felt herself caving in under the attack. It knew her.

"I am the only truth." It was irreverent. "Your *God* has forsaken you!"

The demon discharged the accusation with a force that shook the building's foundation, propelling Samara's body weightlessly into nearby tables and chairs. She braced for the impact, collapsing in a heap of quaking fear. No one noticed. Samara and the dark angel battled in the invisible dimension. She was left to fight this evil alone.

Samara lay motionless on the cold, unwelcoming floor as she watched Tony throw back another beer. All attempts at gaining his attention had proven futile. She was frightened, bruised, and out of options. The longer she engaged, the more she suffered. Maybe the demon was right. God was understandably impervious to her situation. He either could not, or would not, help her now. Why should He? She had done nothing to deserve divine intervention.

Her attacker wanted something that apparently she alone had the ability to provide. Samara had been lured into mortal combat to contend for Tony's soul. But she couldn't imagine why it mattered. She and Tony were no longer married. His future was of no consequence to her. Let him fight his own battles, she thought. Her family had already endured enough pain and suffering to last a lifetime. She just wanted to go home.

Rapid snapshots of her children flashed through her mind. She owed it to them to survive. Whatever it was worth, Samara was ready to concede. There was nothing to lose that was not already lost.

The weapons of our warfare are not carnal, but mighty through God, to the pulling down of strongholds. Samara heard the thought in her head.

It came from another place and was authoritative in its pronouncement. The dark angel's head remained bowed, yet Samara knew intuitively that it had heard what she had heard. The statement didn't come from the foul spirit. She was sure of it. The evil presence appeared suddenly agitated. Something had changed.

A hideous face materialized from beneath the hooded robe, revealing the identity of her accuser. The piercing eyes locked with hers. Samara had never experienced such unbridled hatred directed straight at her. She remained crouched on the floor, pondering her next move. She must stay focused.

"You've lost." The dark angel spoke audibly for the first time.

Samara was both repulsed and mesmerized. The hideous yet strangely intriguing face appeared multi-dimensional. An unnatural fascination tugged at her insides. Something in the dark angel's eyes beckoned to her. She challenged the probing, hypnotic stare. The longer she met its gaze, the stronger the pull. A voice within her shouted, *Resist!*

"Jesus is Lord." The words fell from Samara's lips, surprising both her and the demon. "He is the only truth."

She spoke the words loud and clear. Every syllable reverberated throughout the atmosphere as quickly as she released them. With every utterance came a renewed hope. The dark angel was visibly shaken but stood his ground.

A curious sensation washed over Samara. The pain that had been coursing through her body had disappeared. She suddenly felt as if she could singlehandedly take on an army of demons. It was so amazing she could barely contain herself.

Her movements were slow and deliberate as she stood to her feet. She squared her shoulders, looking her accuser in the eyes. This fight was over.

"*Jesus* is the only truth," she challenged the demon, using his own words.

Without warning and without another word, the evil presence vanished into a concealed darkness.

If I think, "My bed will comfort me, and I will try to forget my misery with sleep," you shatter me with dreams. You terrify me with visions.
—Job 7:13 (NLT)

CHAPTER II

SOMEONE CALLED HER NAME.

"Samara."

"Tony!"

Samara awakened to the sound of her own voice screaming in the night for her ex-husband. She sprang forward, gasping as though she had been pulled from the bottom of the river. The sweat drenched nightgown clung to her shivering body. A cool dampness mopped her creased brow.

Her arms hung limp and heavy at her sides, numb from the lack of circulation. She had been sleeping on her stomach with her arms folded underneath. The prickly needle sensation started at her shoulders and ran straight through to her wrists. She rubbed them vigorously to get the blood flowing. They were cold to the touch.

Through the passing seconds, Samara fought her way back from the horrors of the nightmare to the reality of full consciousness. Echoes of her labored breathing eclipsed the pounding of her stuttering heart. She was no longer dreaming, of that, she was sure. Yet, she could not shake the feeling that someone or *something* was hovering in the shadows. Even now.

"That was just a little bit too real for me." She whispered in the darkness.

Samara sat very still in the middle of the otherwise empty bed, fighting the urge to scream, cry, or both. Her eyes strained against the cloaking blackness. She wasn't sure what she was looking for, but was sure as heck hoping not to find it. Images of demons lurking in dark corners still danced in her brain. At forty-something, she was way too old to be afraid of things that go bump in the night, and yet …

Get it together girl. There are no monsters hiding under the bed or in the closet.

She clutched the bulky comforter with both hands, pulling it to her neck. But it provided little relief against the late night chill, and even less the icy grip of imminent dread.

Why can't I have a few moments of peaceful sleep like everybody else?

Samara raked her fingers through tousled curls as she pondered the meaning of the dream. She unraveled the rubber bands wrapped around her wrist from the previous day and pulled her hair back in a ponytail. Being alone in the dark is one thing. To wake up screaming in the middle of the night is another. Together, it was cruel and unusual punishment.

If this nighttime, made-for-TV drama had anything to do with re-connecting with her ex, she was not interested. She had neither the time nor the inclination to be bothered.

After succumbing to the pain of emotional death by a thousand lashes since the divorce, Samara had figured she would be better off flying low, under the radar. Her life had settled into a mind-numbing, dreary routine. What little desire she might have had for anything resembling a relationship had died. Rigor mortis had set in and she was just fine with that.

She'd admit to the occasional outburst of angry tears and a simmering self-pity every now and again. Overall, her life was uneventful, if not downright boring. The last thing she needed was a resurgence of more "Tony" drama, ad infinitum. He had already cost her too many years of her life—and her finest ones at that. No telling how much damage had been done to the kids. They didn't deserve any more.

Samara groped for the lamp and flipped the switch. It was her best defense against this latest paranoia. The nightlight that doubled as an air freshener wasn't cutting it anymore. The room smelled good, but she needed the kind of light that would dispel the disconcerting darkness and everything skulking in its crevices.

Unfortunately, life didn't look much better with the lights on. The cold harsh truth of her reality was almost as ugly as the nightmare. Unassembled moving boxes lined the perimeter of her bedroom; a cruel reminder that she and the kids were moving out of their beloved home within a few short days. She could just scream, again. This time on purpose.

She wasn't sure how much more of the madness she could take. Everyone had a breaking point, and she reckoned she was pretty close to hers. When she was just a kid, a Sunday school teacher told her that God would not allow His children to suffer beyond their ability to endure the affliction.

"If God allowed it, then you can handle it." She had said.

The teacher was not one to go spouting off stuff that wasn't biblically sound, so Samara figured there had to be some merit of truth in there somewhere. But somebody up there must have gotten their signals mixed, because this was ridiculous.

"Mom?" Her son Nicky called quietly through the half-opened door.

"Come in honey. What are you doing up so late?"

"I couldn't sleep" He stood by the door, his hand resting on the knob. "I was playing with my X Box and thought I heard you calling me. You okay?"

"Yeah, I'm okay—just had a weird dream. I must've been talking in my sleep." Samara offered a weak smile.

"Maybe it's all the stress." He proposed. "You're making yourself crazy trying to do everything yourself."

"There's so much to do. We're talking about packing up twenty years' worth of living in a very big house. I thought I'd have more done by now."

"Mom-Mom said she offered to help out. Why don't you just ask her?"

"That's not a good idea." Samara shook her head. "Your grandmother means well, but I can handle this."

"She said she asked you to come live with her and Pop-Pop."

"And I appreciate the offer, but Mom and I don't get along too well living in the same house. Everything has to be done her way, and we'd end up fighting about every little thing. It's better that I stay with Nana."

It was their first face-to-face conversation in days. Nicky had been avoiding direct contact with Samara since the day they had learned they would have to move out of their house. He stayed locked in his room most of the time, only coming out to eat or use the bathroom. If any words passed between them, it was usually through closed doors.

Nicky entered Samara's bedroom, in no apparent hurry to end the visit. He dropped into the chair by the window and stared out into the darkness. It was a move contrary to his general disposition of late. He typically ran for the hills at the first sign of lengthy dialogue, especially any concerning his family.

Samara threw her legs over the side of the bed, shoving her feet into furry slippers. She knew her children better than they knew themselves. Her son had something on his mind and he had chosen this moment to talk about it. The middle of the night wasn't the best time for a family powwow, but she'd take what she could get. They had a lot of catching up to do. She would tread lightly lest the moment end as abruptly as it began.

"How are things with you?" Samara took her cue.

"Okay, I guess." He did not turn from the window.

"Just okay?"

"What's happening to us?" He blurted. "It's like we've been dismantled, one person at a time. How are we supposed to still be a family after we leave here?"

"Oh, honey." Samara rose from her bed and went to him. "I know this is hard, but we'll be okay. We've survived worse than this, haven't we?"

"I guess so." He didn't seem convinced.

Samara kissed the top of her son's head. Her heart ached for her deeply sensitive child. One moment he's a typical teenager with nothing more pressing than deciding which jeans to wear to the mall. Then, without warning, he's the man of the house. His life had been re-scripted without his permission.

Now, at the tender age of twenty, he was still struggling to find his place. He wanted and needed to move on, but he was worried about leaving her. Samara's anger at Tony rekindled all over again. Their son should not be overly concerned about her welfare. He should be off somewhere having the time of his life.

"Listen," Samara persisted, "we might be moving out of this house, but we're still a family. Besides, you'll be living on campus, and Deb's got her own place now. I would have been in this big old house by myself. At least this way, I'll be with your great-grandmother. We'll be good company for each other."

"But we won't have a place to come home to anymore." He confessed his greatest fear.

There was the whole of the matter. Samara's family tree had been plucked up by the roots, and she was helpless to do anything about it. They would be scattered and replanted. She felt utterly defeated, but was not about to pass her anxiety on to her children. They were innocent victims caught in the crosshairs of life. Their only crime was that they had parents with serious issues.

"Nicky, look at me." Samara faced down her own fears. "Don't you worry about having a place to go. My home is your home, no matter where I live. You know that don't you?"

"I've always known that. It's just that I want you to be okay, and not worry about me anymore."

Samara was overwhelmed by her son's concern. She had been so self-absorbed that she had misread the signals. Nicky hadn't been angry with her, he was afraid.

"Oh honey," She held his gaze, "we're all okay. None of us need ever worry about being homeless. Your grandmother would never see us on the street. If she had her way she'd be driving the U-Haul truck over here, loading it up, and moving us in with them tomorrow."

"That's true." He smiled just a little. "She told Deb and me that we could stay with her and Pop-Pop too, if we wanted."

"See there? Our family may have its very own set of issues, and I do mean *is-shoes*, but we are there for each other when it really matters. The three of us have to spread out for a bit, that's all. We will be a family just the same. You can't get rid of us that easily."

Nicky stood and hugged his mother for the first time in months. Samara looked up at his six-foot-two inch frame and saw relief in his eyes. Her son had been bearing a burden that was not his to carry.

"Thanks, Mom." He kissed her on the cheek.

"Wow, I get a kiss too? I must've hit the jackpot."

"Only at home," Nicky jested, "Never in public."

"I'm not complaining." Samara returned the hug. "And listen, I am so proud of you. Deb and I would've been a little challenged if you hadn't stepped up to the plate when your dad moved out. You took real good care of us."

"It wasn't easy," he jested. "The women in this family are special."

"Like you're the easiest person to get along with?" Samara poked her son. "You are a chore. But I love you anyway."

"I know." He crossed his eyes and wiggled his fingers in his ears the way he had when he was a kid.

"Get out of here child," Samara laughed as she swatted her son out of the room.

She was still smiling when she got back into bed. Having the heart-to-heart with Nicky had brought an unexpected sense of relief. The whole ordeal had taken its toll on all of them. Maybe now there'd be a little less tension in the house. She and Nicky had signed a peace agreement. Now, if she could just drag her stubborn daughter to the table.

"I could smack Tony right in front of his stupid little girlfriend." Samara sucked her teeth. "How dare he disconnect from his responsibilities and leave me to clean up the mess. I don't get to walk away. Why should he?"

She rolled her shoulders to relieve the mounting tension. A hot, soothing bath in the morning would suit her just right. For now, her mind and body needed rest. But she was too afraid to sleep. The sweet flight into the night was just beyond her reach. The darkness held too many frightening possibilities. An unknown enemy had taken up illegal residence in her dreams—stalking, waiting.

Flickering images from this latest dream lingered with pristine clarity. It was akin to watching an upcoming movie preview in slow motion on an old reel-to-reel. Except in this case, it was in living color and the script was unrehearsed. She needed to find a way to make it stop.

This was more than a random, bizarre nightmare. In fact, it had not been the first. She had chosen to ignore the others, chalking them up to a self-diagnosed, post-traumatic stress disorder. Her symptoms matched those that she read on the Internet, exactly. This was a different kind of war, but it was still battle fatigue nonetheless. She knew in her knower that this was not going away without a fight.

It was anybody's guess as to where she'd find the strength for another round.

Maybe she'd run it by her grandmother. She trusted her judgment. In the meantime, a real-life nightmare was staring Samara in the face. Moving her family out of their beloved home would take all the courage she could muster. She would have to face this dilemma alone, just like in the dream.

She stretched her willowy figure beneath the comforter. After three years of divorcee survival camp, she still slept on her side of the bed. Lying in another spot was akin to driving down the wrong side of the road. It just didn't feel right, even if the steering wheel *was* on the other side. She could not bring herself to move from her appointed space of twenty years. It was a perfectly good waste of the king-size bed.

Samara looked over the room that had been her place of refuge. When they first bought the house, they had knocked out a wall and added on extra space just for her. She had hired an interior designer to help turn the massive room into a charming, multipurpose hideaway. The consultant came highly recommended, and was well worth the added expense.

They had picked up an old mahogany desk at an antique shop in the artsy section of town. The vintage desk sat cattycornered on an oval shaped oriental rug, and served as her office on those days she had worked from home. A Queen Anne table and chair marked the reading area, where Samara spent most of her time with her kindle, or staring mindlessly through the floor-to-ceiling windows. The big bed sat in the middle of the floor, strategically dividing the designated areas.

This room was where Samara would come whenever she needed peace and quiet. It was her favorite place to be. When she closed the door, everyone understood that she was not to be bothered. If you dared enter, it was at your own risk. Now it would belong to someone else.

She fluffed the feathery pillows and propped herself against the headboard. Getting a good night's sleep was turning out to be a rare event. There would be no rest for the weary tonight. She would stay awake and deal with this until the sun came up.

God help me. Samara grabbed the television remote.

The silent presence prepared to make its exit. He had been dismissed. Mission accomplished.

*Are they not all spirits engaged in special service, sent on assignment
for the sake of those who are going to inherit salvation?*
—Hebrews 1:14 (LEB)

Chapter III

L ARIEL MOVED DEFTLY THROUGH the sphere that intertwined the earth's inhabitants with angels of both light and darkness. It still amazed the guardian that most humans scoff at the mere suggestion of another kingdom operating juxtaposed to theirs. The parallel dimension is invisible to the undiscerning, but is nonetheless very real. More relevant, in fact.

He hastened on his mission. The telltale sulfuric vapor announced the presence of enemy soldiers tracking him at a respectable distance. From what Lariel could determine, at least a hundred pairs of jaundiced, cat-like eyes dotted the darkness. The lowly henchmen had followed him from the subject's house, clearly on a fact-finding mission.

The swooshing of monstrous wings flapping through the night did little to intimidate Lariel. He would just as soon destroy the hideous vermin. But this was not the time. The squadron would meet with its destiny soon enough.

He had been ordered to return to his command post where Gabriel and the others awaited his report. They had gathered in the attic of an abandoned church. The building was long vacant, but the heartfelt prayers and hymns of years gone by still resonated in the atmosphere. The angelic hosts savored every bit of the harmonious splendor. If the humans only knew— nothing was ever lost.

Similar stations scattered the area. A homeless shelter, an overcrowded children's home, and a fledgling nursing facility provided more than adequate cover for the heavenly beings. The hosts considered it a high honor. The inhabitants were precious in the sight of the Highest and in theirs as well.

"Lariel, I rejoice in your return, my brother." Gabriel greeted him upon arrival.

The archangel's posture was unassuming, his authority was not. Lariel raised his sword to salute the highest-ranking officer. Gabriel's involvement could mean only one thing—this was not business as usual. Lariel was pleased to be on the same assignment as his compatriot. It had been many years since they had fought together.

Gabriel's brigade of warring angels gathered throughout the church in small clusters, preparing for the command. The more experienced soldiers stationed themselves along the outside perimeter; warding off unwanted interference. Many marveled at the honor of fighting alongside such high-ranking officers. Others wondered at the gravity of the mission. It was not often that they were selected to assist in high profile operations.

"To what do we owe this honor, Gabriel?" Lariel sat facing the archangel.

"The Deceiver has stepped up his attack against your human." Gabriel's smile disappeared.

"Indeed. His top henchmen have targeted her."

"This mission has drawn quite a bit of attention."

"From both sides." Lariel glanced around the room. "A little curious, wouldn't you say?"

"I would. And it appears that we are not alone in our curiosity."

"We are not." Lariel nodded toward the stain glass windows. "An envoy of at least a hundred enemy troops followed me here."

"We sensed their arrival." Gabriel unsheathed his sword. "They dare not engage."

"No, my brother," Lariel motioned for his friend to put away his weapon. "They don't intend to."

A heightened sense of urgency permeated the building. It was unmistakably apparent that the stakes were high.

"Even so, the mission tonight was a success." Gabriel assured Lariel.

"The demon confronted her directly. He was using her to provoke me."

"True." Gabriel conceded. "But our orders are to protect, not interfere."

"I do not question my orders, but I cannot help but wonder why this human has drawn so much attention. She's not yet strong enough to withstand the attack on her own."

"Whatever the reason, the Deceiver is taking no chances." Gabriel looked intently upon his fellow soldier. "Neither shall we."

"And what of her family?" Lariel submitted.

"Michael has instructed that they are never to be without full coverage from here out. The Deceiver will most likely attempt to use them as a distraction. But we are not ignorant of his devices."

A few hundred feet in the distance, enemy forces kept themselves at bay on strict orders from the master, himself. This bode well for the demonic contingent. They were all too familiar with the occupants of the church and had no intention of inviting themselves to the little get-together. Prince Michael was not present, but his involvement was duly noted. Gabriel was obviously heading up the operation. His special warrior division guarded the command post.

Any fool knows that you don't mess with archangels—not even on a good day. Better to sit this one out.

For our struggle is not against flesh and blood, but against the rulers, against the authorities, against the powers of this dark world and against the spiritual forces of evil in the heavenly realms.
—Ephesians 6:12 (NIV)

Chapter Iv

Samara peeked through the slats of the venetian blinds. The sky was a beautiful shade of blue, the sun was shining, and the birds were chirping. It was a typical, late summer morning. Except for one thing—the sheriff would be there soon. Today was the day they would deliver the official notice to vacate the premises.

She glanced up the street, almost expecting to see a cavalry charging down her block on white horses, waving the papers in their hands. They would dismount in unison, march up to her porch, and nail the obtrusive announcement to her front door.

A pained smile etched the corners of her mouth. It might as well happen that way. The Sheriff Sale procedure was no less invasive. Get out or be put out. It doesn't get any more humiliating than that. Her neighborhood was her world, and everyone would know that she had failed miserably—yet again.

Her attorney had suggested that she file for bankruptcy in hopes of securing a last-minute reversal of sentence. What she got was an even uglier credit score. The attempts to save the house had only served to prolong the inevitable. Samara had exhausted every perceivable option. They had to go. Some other family would be living in their precious home.

The bay window had been her favorite place to sit and ponder. But, no more. She must hurry. The kids were probably done packing. She did not want them there when the sheriff arrived. They deserved this last vestige of dignity. They had lived in the same house for nearly twenty years, establishing lifelong friendships. The close-knit community was a part of them—a living, breathing organism. They invaded each other's homes for everything from a cup of sugar to sleepovers and prom nights.

Samara heaved a weary sigh as she turned from her distraction. Her spacious three-story colonial was in total disarray—from the finished basement that housed their game room and dust-ridden exercise equipment, to the upper attic that stored only God knows what. Everything was strewn about, waiting for somebody to make sense of the chaos. She probably should have asked for help, but this was nobody's business. Nobody's but theirs.

Besides, she was in no mood for listening to misplaced, overused Bible verses declaring that this will all somehow work out for her good. What good could possibly come from this? Her life was unraveling at the speed of light. Everything she had worked so hard to build was slipping through her fingers. These were her family and her home.

God had blessed her with both. She had believed that once, but truth was so elusive now. The last thing she or the kids needed was one more pound-cake-carrying, phonily smiling, positive-thought-of-the-day-quoting, know-it-all. Not to mention the nosy busybodies with their obnoxious meddling. No thanks.

It was all so surreal, like having an out-of-body experience. One minute your life is on track—just the way you planned it. Then, without warning, you watch helplessly as the pieces tumble at your feet, tripping you up like a juggling act gone badly. Samara wondered how positive those same people would be if they woke up and discovered *their* family, *their* house, and *their* jobs gone.

She eyed the empty U-Haul boxes.

"Let's do this." She approached the packing receptacles with defiant resolve.

They would transport the remnants of her broken life to their temporary holding places. Most of the household contents were headed for storage. Their treasured possessions would soon be collecting dust in some sixteen-by-ten foot concrete hole-in-the-wall. The rest was going with her to her maternal grandmother's home in West Philly. Every trace of her family's existence would be eliminated. They were, and now they are no more.

At least she would have a chance to spend time with her nana. Samara had spent many childhood summers in her grandparents' house, eating sumptuous meals, and listening to stories of days gone by. She was returning the same way she left—by herself. The last thing she wanted was to dump her issues on someone else. Nevertheless, she needed a place to stay, and her nana needed help with the big house, especially now that Grand Pop was gone.

Samara could already smell the peach cobbler baking in the oven. A healthy dose of some good, old-fashioned comfort might be just what the doctor ordered. Not having to cook for a change was icing on the cake; or in this case—cool whip on the cobbler.

The matter was settled. She was moving out of the Jersey suburb, back into the city, much to the expressed disappointment of her mother and stepfather.

"Why won't you move in with us?" Her mother had said. "You know we have plenty of space."

"It's an easier commute, Mom." It was the best excuse Samara could conjure up.

"Why burden your grandmother?"

Samara's mother generally spoke in phrases that ended with question marks.

"Nana says it's not a burden. She has the space."

"And we don't? What about the kids? Where will they go? They need to have some sense of security, especially now. I think you're being a bit selfish."

"I'm not being selfish. Nana is in that big house by herself and needs help. The kids are okay."

"She's my mother, don't you think I know what she needs better than you? And don't be so sure about the kids. They have been through a lot in a short space of time. I told them that they could come and stay with us, but they won't come without you."

"I know. Nicky told me."

"And?" Her mother pressed the issue.

"And I think they've decided to do what's best for them right now. They're not kids anymore Mom. We can't make them do anything they don't want to."

The conversation had ended on a sour note, as usual.

Her parents loved her and wanted to offer their help. She didn't doubt that. But Samara knew what was best for her family, whether her mother believed that or not. The last thing her kids needed was to move in with their grandparents. They need space to figure things out. Moving in with them would only further complicate matters.

"Hey." Her daughter's voice startled her.

"How long were you standing there?" She turned and faced her youngest child.

"Not long. You okay?" Deborah searched her mother's eyes.

"I'll be done eventually," Samara avoided her daughter's probing stare, "as soon as I figure out how to work these boxes."

Maximus, their German shepherd, made his grand entrance behind Deborah. The dog had been a Christmas present for the kids when they were all toddlers. They had begged Tony and her all year long for a pet. Tony was gung ho, but Samara was not so sure. It was hard enough cleaning up behind a husband and three kids. But she finally gave in, and now she couldn't imagine their lives without Maximus. He was as much a part of the family as her children.

"Need some help?" Deborah grabbed a carton.

"No. Are you finished packing?"

Samara watched her daughter effortlessly assemble the cardboard contraption.

"I'm done. Nicky left with his stuff. His roommate picked him up."

"He could've at least said good bye."

"I think he's taking this really hard. He said he'll call you later." Deborah mastered another box. "His fraternity is having a move-in party on campus today. You really look like you could use some help."

"I'm okay." Samara turned back to her box. "Just make sure you haven't forgotten anything. Put your name on all of the packing labels. Your stuff goes on the truck last."

With that, Deborah retreated to the safety of her bedroom, gently closing the door behind her. Maximus trotted to where Samara stood, looking at her as if to say, *what do we do now?*

Samara put the empty box aside.

"I know Max." She scratched the dog's ears. "That didn't go too well."

She hadn't meant to be so abrupt. There was so much she wanted to say to her daughter. She longed to wrap her arms around her as she had when she was a little girl. Deborah needed to know that everything would be all right. But any attempt at having any meaningful conversation generally deteriorated to uncontrollable shouting matches. Samara just did not feel like it.

Maximus jumped on the bed and settled in for a nap. His age was beginning to affect his movement, but he could still get around pretty well.

Samara reached unconsciously for the gold chain hanging around her neck. On it, a beautiful antique charm held her birthstone, the stones of her three children, and a pendant with the word *"Mom."* The kids had given it to her as a Mother's Day gift. It had been TJ's idea to have the necklace specially made. He had had a part time job and had wanted to surprise her. Their father had ended up footing most of the bill, but she was proud of her children for their efforts.

"This way, you'll always have us with you." TJ had said, as he placed the chain around her neck.

He had died exactly one week later in a violent car crash. His death had been so hard on everyone, but especially the kids. They had looked up to their big brother. It did not make sense that he was gone. Samara wanted to talk about it with Deborah and Nicky, but they would not let her in.

Her children were changing right before her eyes. She loved them more than life itself, but she wasn't so sure she liked what they were becoming. Deborah spent more time with her boyfriend than at home. Nicky seemed a little more approachable since their last talk, but essentially he had retreated to the safety of his friends. Nothing about their lives made sense anymore. The rules of engagement had been rewritten.

Are you there God? Carest thou not that we perish?

Samara collected the remaining, yet-to-be-assembled boxes, dragging them behind her to the walk-in closet. She had procrastinated long enough. Cleaning out closets was her least favorite thing. She swore hers had a life all its own. How else could she explain the growing number of assorted items jammed beyond normal capacity? Some of the clothing had been hidden in the deep portals for years. They still had tags on them.

If there were such things as monsters in closets, they wouldn't stand a chance in here, she thought. Everything imaginable rested in the nooks and crannies of the double-door continuum. She didn't even remember purchasing half the things lining the shelves. It was a scary mess. It was a definite possibility that she had violated every safety code known to human and spirit-kind alike.

Her first line of defense was to attack the mountain of shoeboxes stacked and separated by style and color. Even Imelda Marcos would laud such a collection. Samara cleared a path to the clothing rack and began the arduous task of maneuvering the tangled hangers. She would just as soon toss the hanging clothes into the boxes. Then she would have a bigger mess, if that were even possible.

As she navigated her exit from the decidedly claustrophobic space, a déjà vu moment arrested her attention. Samara froze mid-stride. It felt like she had done this before.

What is it about this living nightmare that could possibly be so familiar?

She searched her brain for a possible trigger. Then it came to her. She had awakened from another weird dream several nights back. It had left her feeling anxious and afraid. She couldn't remember why. The particulars had faded in and out like an elusive lover. She had not been able to make sense of the puzzling images, yet the nagging feeling had haunted her—as if it were important that she remember.

And the great dragon was cast out, that old serpent, called the Devil and Satan, which deceiveth the whole world: he was cast out into the earth, and his angels were cast out with him.
—Revelation 12:9 (KJV)

Chapter V

"What have you to say for yourself, Thumar?"

"I did as I was commanded, my lord." The dark angel squirmed ever so slightly.

"Did you, now?" Mastema, the commander and arch demon, rose slowly from his bejeweled seat located in the center of the interrogation room.

Thumar kept silent. He did not presume to speak again. It was a rare privilege to be summoned to this domain: A privilege, or a death sentence. The master's private quarters lay just beyond the heavily guarded gates. Angels of his rank were scarcely, if ever, granted access. The soldiers posted at the entrance eyed Thumar from across the room with unmasked contempt. This was going to be interesting.

Mastema rose to full stature, prompting enviable stares from the lower-ranking officers. His massive, dark frame engulfed the room. Undulating ripples of pure evil oozed from his pores, seeping into every unfilled space. Razor-sharp metal scales clinked in unison as he extended his gargantuan wings for full effect. The performance was not lost on his audience.

"Your human outsmarted you," the arch demon mocked Thumar, eliciting crude remarks from the guards.

"She had help." Thumar began his defense. "The prince ..."

"I know who was there, you fool!" Mastema hissed.

Mastema approached Thumar with the stealth of a hungry panther. The attending officers and guards gave their full attention to the scene playing out before them. Their commander seemed more incensed than usual.

Again, Thumar kept silent. He wondered what this human had done to provoke direct confrontation from their ranks. She seemed too confused and ill equipped to warrant this kind of attention. The wretched creature was clearly out of her league. Yet, how did he explain the appearance of Prince Michael? The archangel had not directly interfered, but had no doubt given the command to Lariel. Either way, this was no small thing.

"Your orders were to gain a confession concerning the spouse." Mastema's words dripped with venom. "She was to deny the existence of her *God*."

"She was about to concede. I had her where I wanted her."

"Then explain your sudden retreat! You were not to leave until the seeds of doubt and failure were firmly planted in her mind."

Mastema drew closer to Thumar. Close enough to smell the fear. Thumar dared not challenge the commander's allegations. To do so would mean certain annihilation. He determined to keep his head bowed. A display of humility might be enough to assuage Mastema's displeasure.

"My lord," Thumar continued his descent, "I believe the human was fully dissuaded concerning any attempts at redeeming the soul of her former spouse. She questioned her *own* faith."

Thumar awaited the arch demon's response. He did not wait long.

"You incompetent moron!" Mastema's sword found its mark, slashing the side of Thumar's face with effortless precision. "Your human has obviously been chosen for some great task that will most assuredly be perilous to our cause! That blasted prince was not on a social visit!"

Thumar felt the warm blood trickling down his marred face, but he did not make a sound, nor change his posture. If he so much as flinched, Mastema would finish him off. Even if Thumar were deliriously insane and were to consider drawing his own sword, the guards would demolish him for the sport of it. They watched from across the room in hopeful anticipation.

"Why did you dismiss yourself before completing your assignment?"

Thumar had no satisfying answer. If he admitted to the defeat, he'd be turned over to the guards for their recreational pleasure. He'd only further infuriate the commander by insisting that he had accomplished some measure of victory. That would guarantee a fate far worse than death.

"Do you dare disrespect me, imp?" Mastema grew impatient.

"My lord, I mean no disrespect."

"Answer my question!"

"I thought it best to abort the mission," Thumar pleaded. "The Word was present."

"Were you afraid, mighty warrior?"

The guards smirked, even if a little uncomfortably. Secretly, each knew that they would have done the same. They had heard the horror stories of fallen comrades who had underestimated the putrid humans. The little creatures were fragile and weak, but the Word was always watching over them—empowering them. It was far better for the fallen angels to face the wrath of their commander.

"The human was protected," Thumar insisted. "Lariel would not have allowed me to finish her off without direct confrontation."

Mastema sniggered under his breath. He and Lariel had met previously under similar circumstances. The guardian had bested him, but that was then. The arch demon would not be such an easy mark this time. The Deceiver had personally taken him under his wing and trained him in special warfare. As a result, he had been promoted to chief commander. Mastema had obliterated many hopefuls to get to this position.

"Ah, yes." Mastema circled Thumar like a vulture closing in on its prey. "Lariel has made it known that he is personally involved. He is quite the formidable opponent, to most."

"I believe I can eliminate Lariel, if given another opportunity," Thumar appealed to the commander's loathing of the guardian.

"And so you shall."

Mastema struck Thumar from behind, sending him crashing to the ground. Thumar cowered in what he hoped was a convincing act of submission. He would save his energy for the right moment. Another time.

"Perhaps we can extract some usefulness out of you after all," Mastema sneered. "Your human has no awareness of her guardian?"

"No, my lord. She doesn't appear to know that he exists."

"Then you must keep her distracted and confused. She must not discover that she is protected."

"Lariel will know."

"Perhaps you will be granted the opportunity to confront him after all." Mastema smirked.

Thumar gathered himself and rose to his feet. He bowed low before the arch demon, stealing a direct glance for the first time. He was not surprised to discover the mutual loathing and distrust in the eyes of his commander.

"Your servant is grateful for another opportunity to prove his loyalty." Thumar feigned allegiance.

"I'm so sure." Mastema turned away in disgust "You're dismissed."

The guards escorted Thumar out of the interrogation room in a less than friendly manner, slamming the gate behind him. The captain of the guards approached Mastema.

"My lord, shall we trail the infidel?"

"Yes." Mastema grinned at the soldiers. "Keep yourselves under cover. Thumar must not know that he is under surveillance."

"And Lariel?"

"The guardian will know you're there, but he is too wise to make his move just yet. He won't waste his time on the likes of Thumar."

Mastema wiped his sword clean of the demon's blood; relishing the moment that he and Lariel would meet again.

"Give the order for the soldier assigned to the spouse to turn up the heat."

"At your command, master."

Mastema let loose a stream of obscenities, incensing those occupying the room with vile anticipation. The smell of warfare filled his nostrils. A battle of epic proportions was brewing in the atmospheres. He could feel it. They all could.

We are troubled on every side, yet not distressed;
we are perplexed, but not in despair.
—2 Corinthians 4:8 (KJV)

Chapter VI

THE CELL PHONE VIBRATED on the dresser.

Not now.

"Que pasa, Mommy?" It was her best friend, Lourdes Mooney; known affectionately to all as "Lu."

"Hey." Samara lowered her body to the hardwood floor, draping the clothed hangers over her lap.

"I won't keep you. Just wanted to see if you needed anything while I'm out and about."

"I'm okay." Samara loved her friend, but she could be windy.

"How are the kids holdin' up?"

"I guess they're okay, but you know how it goes. They're not really saying much. The most I get these days are sound bites. I don't know what to do to make this any less painful than it already is. I feel like I've failed them."

"Don't go blaming yourself, girl. Listen, you didn't buy that house by yourself, and you certainly can't afford to keep it now that you're unemployed."

"I know, but the grownups are supposed to be the ones that have their acts together."

"It's not your fault. They know that."

"I hope so. Nicky and I finally had a civil conversation the other night. It was a pleasant moment of sanity. He seemed a little better afterwards. I wish somebody would convince *me*."

"That's what you have me for." Lourdes switched gears. "Is Nicky still moving on campus?"

"Yup," Samara lamented. "He left this afternoon."

"And Deborah?"

Samara leaned her head against the closet door, shifting her weight on the unyielding parquet. What could she say about her headstrong daughter?

"Deb is moving in with her boyfriend."

Lu caught her breath. "*Mira! No esta lista!* You can't let her do that!"

"She's eighteen. I can't stop her."

"She's only a baby. What does she know about living with a man?"

"To hear her tell it, she knows more than I think she does."

"She said that?" Lu's voice was nearing second soprano range.

"Yes, she did. We were fighting, and she was angry. I know she didn't mean it, but she really believes that they know what they're getting into. I guess they'll have to learn the hard way, like the rest of us."

"Wow. Do you at least know where they're moving to?"

"She gave me an address. The movers are dropping her things off first. It's not the worst neighborhood, but it's not the best either." Samara pictured the apartment building in her mind. "I guess I'll have to work up the nerve to ask for an invite."

"It's a lot for you to digest. You sure you don't want me to come help?" Lu pressed her friend.

"Thanks, but we need to do this as a family." Samara closed her eyes, fighting back fatigue and remorse.

"I hear you." Lu didn't miss a beat. "Guess who I saw last night?"

Samara's heart triple somersaulted. Here it comes. She already knew the answer, and she wasn't ready to talk about it. Not even with her best friend.

"Lu please, this is not the best time for the latest Tony report."

"Girl, I saw him with *her* at Whole Foods." Lu would not be denied. This was too juicy.

"I already know about the girlfriend." Samara shifted again, shutting the bedroom door with her foot.

Another well-meaning friend had given her the 411. Samara was not interested in the sordid details of Tony's love life. Unfortunately, that did not stop the influx of up-to-the-minute breaking news. Her friends considered it their moral obligation to notify her of every ex-husband sighting. Having a cell phone only made it worse.

Tony medicated himself with multiple relationships. That was his way. But that knowledge did little to lessen the anxiety of constantly hearing about it. The calls and text messages came at all hours of the day and night.

Samara prepared for more nerve-wracking gossip. Lu meant well, but this was no different from any of the other calls. She rested her head against the closet door, wishing she could hit the "ignore" button.

"They had two small children with them—looking like the picture-perfect family." Lu sucked her teeth.

"Whatever." Samara massaged her temples with her free hand.

"He pretended not to see me, but I know he did. I wanted to march right up to them and force him to speak. It would've served him right."

"It doesn't matter anymore."

"Yes it does. Have you seen her?"

"No, and I'm praying that I won't. It would be my luck to run into them on a bad hair day, when I'm wearing the most raggedy outfit in my closet and no makeup. I don't think I can handle that right now."

"I wouldn't worry about that. She's not *hardly* cute, with her man-stealing self. I don't know what he sees in her."

It didn't matter. Whatever Tony saw in his latest girlfriend was enough to keep him from coming back to his family. And to Samara.

"Sam?"

"Yes."

"You okay?"

"No." Samara felt like she was suffocating.

"I'm here for you."

"I know, sweetie. Let me go. The movers will be here soon."

"Call me when you come to your senses. You need help. Love you."

Samara didn't bother hitting the button to end the call. She threw the phone across the room with every bit of strength she could muster. She wanted to smash it against the wall so that it broke into little bitsy pieces. Instead, it bounced and landed safely on the blanket-covered bed, next to Maximus. He opened his eyes but did not move.

"Figures," she whispered.

Just when she thought it was safe to wade into the water, somebody cued the theme song from the movie "Jaws." The whole mess was swallowing her alive. She thought she was getting better about the whole "girlfriend" thing, but obviously, she was not. Her heart still raced at the mention of it. She longed for the day when she'd have no reaction whatsoever.

Samara dragged herself across the room and crawled into the middle of her bed, knocking the phone to the floor.

"Off, Max." She shoved the big dog.

Salty tears trickled through the corners of her eyes and down her face. Then the levee burst. Heart wrenching sobs racked her tired body. The burgeoning heartache of her son's death and the divorce escaped as a wail through her lips. She had been the self-appointed rock of Gibraltar for what was left of her family. But it was too much to carry alone. All the fight was gone.

"I can't do this anymore." Samara moaned.

Failure and remorse scratched the edges of her psyche like sharpened talons. There was nowhere to hide. She succumbed to the encroaching sadness.

Maximus trotted to where Samara lay crying. He plopped down close to the bed and did not move until she had fallen asleep. Only then, did he relocate to the foot of the bed and resume his nap.

* * *

"Hello?" Lourdes poked her head through the door.

"Lu?" Samara sat up in the bed.

Several hours had passed since she had cried herself to sleep. The room was dark. Lourdes flipped on the ceiling light.

"I knew I should come. You're strong, but you're no superwoman."

"Why is God punishing me?" Samara choked back fresh tears.

Lourdes sat on the edge of the bed, clutching her friend's hands.

"Look at me. You know God's not punishing you."

"Don't sit there and tell me God's not punishing me, because *this* doesn't make sense." Samara snatched her hands from her friends'. "My life is an absolute mess."

"You know better than that. Everybody's got her own share of drama. Nobody's life is perfect, no matter what it looks like from the outside."

"I'm not asking for perfect. I just want normal."

"Come on. Let's pray." Lu stood to her feet.

"Pray about what?" Samara challenged. "My husband left me. He's flaunting his new girlfriend all over town. I have to move my children out of the only home they have ever known. I hate what this is doing to them. It's not fair."

"You know kids." Lourdes consoled her friend. "They're resilient. They'll come around."

"Will they? Their brother's death was traumatizing enough. Our memories of TJ are tied to this house. Then they had to deal with the divorce. Now they have to leave here feeling disconnected from everything that made them feel safe. My whole family has disintegrated."

"It could be worse."

"You're kidding me, right?" Samara stared back through bloodshot eyes. "Deborah's moving in with some kid I don't even like and Nicky just started speaking to me again."

"At least all of you have some place to go. You have the support of your family."

"Really? My mother thinks I am incapable of making a single, sound decision. She might be right. There's nothing good about my life right now. Nothing."

"Don't talk that way. At least let me pray with you." Lu pleaded with her friend.

"You pray." Samara's voice cracked with exhaustion. "I don't have the strength to believe anymore. My prayers don't get answered."

"I understand." Lu spun on her heels.

"No." Samara turned her back, pulling the blanket over her head. "You don't."

Lourdes grabbed a box and began packing up her best friend's house without another word.

*The Lord said to Satan, "Very well, then, everything he has
is in your hands, but on the man himself do not lay a finger."
Then Satan went out from the presence of the LORD.
—Job 1:12 (NIV)*

Chapter VII

BERNAEL LICKED HIS LIPS. This was going to be easier than he had anticipated. He rubbed his scaled claws together in slobbering anticipation. The dumb human was so self-absorbed; he never considered that his life had been sabotaged. But then, why would he? The worm really believed that abandoning his family was *his* idea. *Stupid, stupid creatures. They honestly think they are in control of their own destiny.*

The demon slithered through the hallway, turning into the bedroom. He would be right there when the loathsome soul turned on his computer. Bernael had a few choice sites of interest to "suggest" to the brainless human. Of course, the dimwit would think it was entirely his choice. How laughable.

He settled in for what looked to be a most eventful evening. *Mastema will be pleased.*

* * *

Anthony Daniels, Sr. paced the length of his living room with acquired military precision. Once a marine, always a marine.

"Semper Fi." He whispered. "Always faithful. Yeah, right."

The smell of fresh cut grass filtered through the screened window, where his mother, Gloria Daniels, was hanging curtains she'd made especially for him.

"It looks like a single man lives here," she had said. "It needs a woman's touch."

In Tony's mind, his apartment wasn't the only thing that needed a woman's touch. He grabbed a cold beer from the cooler. His mother glanced his way, but remained silent.

Tony brought the bottle to his mouth. The brew was cold and satisfying. He wondered what his ex-wife would say if she saw him. Samara had never let him drink anything stronger than root beer in the house. Indulging in libational activities had been a source of contention with her. Fortunately for him, she had never found the private stash he had kept in the garage. His man-cave. He missed that house.

Why should he care what Samara thought anyway? That was then and this is now. It was time to be true to himself. Performing the same act of the same play had become old and stale. He had grown weary of living a double life. If people didn't like the person he was, then that was their problem.

There was no need to try to convince Samara that he would change. He wasn't so sure it was possible anymore. As far as Tony was concerned, he was beyond help. The full-blown addiction was out of control. He felt dirty when he indulged and guilt ridden when he didn't. It was a lose–lose situation.

Sometimes it felt like an unseen force was behind the curtains pulling his strings. But that sound like a copout that nobody would ever believe. He cursed softly under his breath. His mother pretended not to hear.

"You're pacing, sweetheart." She called him back from the edge.

"Habit." Tony replied.

"You want to talk about it?"

There was no sense trying to convince his mother that everything was okay. She knew better and was most likely the only person who really cared. Tony figured he might as well have a go at it.

"I haven't heard from the kids." It was not what he had intended to say.

"So we're finally going to talk about this? I was wondering how long it would take."

"I guess it's bothering me more than I thought."

"That's understandable. We all have our own ways of protecting ourselves from life's disappointments. Did you honestly believe that you had the right to walk away from your children? You need to contact them. It's been too long."

"I'm not about to call the house. They'd see my name on the caller ID and let it go to voicemail. Or it would be just my luck to have Samara pick up the phone. I'm sure she has more than a few choice words for me. It's my fault they have to move out."

Tony drained the first bottle of beer and grabbed another from his diminishing stash. He had known about the foreclosure for some time now. The people from the bank had contacted him several months back because he was the primary borrower.

They wanted to know what his intentions were. He never knew there were so many options to consider.

The representative had said that Samara wanted to sell the house. All Tony had to do was to sign the paperwork and fax it back to them. But he never did. Somewhere in his atrophied state of mind, he really believed that he would come up with the back payments. It was the least he could do after disappearing on his family. Now it was too late. He would never forgive himself.

"Nope." He restated his position to his mother. "Can't do that. I'm not calling the house."

"Well, if it's really the kids you want to talk to," Gloria peeped over the rim of her glasses, "why don't you call their cell phones? Or send them text messages. It's better than nothing."

"Since when did you become so modernized?" Tony smirked at his mother. "I had to beg you to start carrying your Blackberry. It stayed in the box it came in for one whole year, unused. And what do you know about texting?"

"Just because I wasn't using it doesn't mean I didn't know how to. Besides, that is how my grandchildren prefer to communicate. They have been texting me ever since they knew my phone was working. It was either that, or I'd have to call them, leave a message, and then wait to hear back. I'm too old to be waiting around for that."

"At least they're communicating with you."

"Stop being so hard on yourself, sweetheart; you didn't kill the Pope."

"I abandoned them, Mom. That doesn't exactly qualify me for Father of the Year."

"They're not little kids anymore. Things happen. They get that."

"Yeah, but in this case I'm the bad guy. God only knows what their mother has been telling them. Not that I blame her. I accept full responsibility for what I've done and all, but it doesn't mean I don't love my own children."

"So what do you intend to do about it?" Gloria placed the last curtain ring in the pleated slot. "Go, or get off the pot."

"I'm open to suggestions at this point."

"Maybe you should make the first move and let the chips fall where they may. Don't you think they care about what's going on with you? You're their father."

"I wouldn't know what to say." Tony continued pacing. "They're not the same kids they were three years ago. Too much has changed."

"But they're still your children. How about letting them know you love them? That's a good a place to start. Children need to know that their parents are there for them, no matter what. Never underestimate the power of a father's love."

Tony paced from the kitchen to the living room and back again. It was the angry march of an absentee father. Three years of birthdays, holidays, and special occasions had come and gone. His mother had kept him informed of every event, just so he'd have some kind of connection. It was better than nothing but not a whole lot.

For some reason, he had expected to wake up one day with a newfound courage to face his past. A month had turned into a year; then two, then three. He had never intended for this much time to pass by. But as time went on, the prospect of reconciling with his children seemed farfetched.

"I keep hoping that something will happen to make this easier." Tony peered into the beer bottle as if the answer were inside. "It's probably too late."

"Nonsense. As long as there is breath in your body, it is never too late. Give them a call. What's the worst that can happen?"

"They can hang up when they hear my voice, or maybe not answer at all."

"So you'll leave a voice message, or better yet, send a text." It was Gloria's turn to smirk at her son.

Tony chuckled at the thought of his mother actually sending text messages. He could picture her fussing at the screen every time the spell-checker changed a word. That's his mother. He tossed the empty beer bottle in the recycle container and moseyed into the living room.

It only took a few short strides to reach the epicenter. He crossed the room and plopped onto the sofa. It sagged under his one hundred eighty pound muscular physique. The poor excuse for a couch had been passed down from one bachelor to another, and had seen better days. Although Tony could not imagine how long ago that must have been. The television was the only thing that really mattered. He would sit on the floor and watch it if he had to.

There wasn't much else to the small apartment. The kitchenette had barely enough room to maneuver. Not that he did much KP duty. His mother used the stove whenever she stopped by for one of her visits. That was it. Most of his meals were taken from the freezer to the microwave to the living room. The dinette set with the side flaps and two chairs served as the place to dump his keys and the mail. It wasn't plush, but it was his.

The bedroom was his favorite. It held the nicest furniture in the place. His parents had given him the matching bed and dresser set as a house-warming gift. Tony had refused to accept it at first, but they would be insulted if he returned it.

"You're a grown man." His father had said. "You can't very well sleep on the floor. Besides, it's just taking up space in our house."

So he had kept it. The computer desk and chair were his gifts to himself. They rounded out the room quite nicely. He considered it his multipurpose area. It was the first time in his adult life that he didn't have to share his personal space with anyone. Sometimes he felt a little guilty about that; but it was what it was. You take the good with the bad.

"Tony, honey," his mother interrupted his thoughts," hand me the other curtain over there on the couch."

He grabbed it off the back of the sofa and took it to her.

"Thanks honey." An odd expression flickered across her face.

"You okay?" He knew he should not have let her hang those curtains. "Gettin' tired?"

"No, no. I'm just …" She held the curtain midair, "feeling a little strange."

"Something wrong?"

"Help me down." Gloria reached for her son's hand.
Tony guided his mother down the stepladder.
"Rest a minute. I can hang the other panel later."
"I'm not tired." She lowered herself on to the sofa.
"Did you take your medicine today?"
"It's not that." She was obviously shaken.
"Then what?"
"I wish I knew."

The angel of God said to me in the dream,
"Jacob." I answered, "Here I am."
—Genesis 31:11 (NIV)

Chapter VIII

"Samara?" Anna Morton called through the closed door.

"You can come in." Samara propped herself on her elbows to greet her grandmother.

"You hungry, sweetheart? You haven't eaten all day."

"I'm okay. I'll grab something later"—a lie on both counts.

"I left a plate in the oven for you." Anna kissed her granddaughter's forehead.

"Thanks, Nana."

"You know I'm here for you if you need me." She turned to leave. "You're not in this alone."

"I know."

Samara loved her Nana Anna more than anyone. She was the only person on God's green earth who had a clue.

"I want everything to be just right for you, Sweet Pea," her nana had said.

She had decorated the guest room in Samara's favorite color. They had picked out curtains together at their favorite home decorating store. It matched the new carpet and freshly painted walls.

"This will be your very own private sanctuary. You'll be just fine."

If only that were true, Samara ruminated. Her grandmother meant well, but she couldn't remember what real peace felt like anymore. She was now a card-carrying, fee paid member of the "Divorced and Lost Everything" club, which apparently reduces your social status. It was okay for her ex to be sporting around town with his latest conquest. After all, he is the newest eligible bachelor. As for Samara, well ... she was the one "left behind." Nobody had told her about *that* cute little double standard.

"Bunch of hypocrites," Samara mumbled under her breath.

Did anyone care to hear her side of the story, at least? Her house had been procured by the bank. Their furniture and other prized possessions had been given to family and friends, or stored away. She was sure to be hiding her beloved car from the repo guy soon—very soon. Her children rarely, if ever, returned her calls. She'd been relegated to communication by text only. And for the *piece de résistance*, she had downsized from a double door walk-in to a *real* closet. A person could take only so much!

She and the kids had left their precious home as inconspicuously as they could. It was hard to do in broad daylight. A few of their closest friends had helped load the truck and deliver their things to various destinations. It took several trips to empty out the big house. After the last stitch of furniture was gone, Samara did the final walk-through with tears streaming down her face. This was not the way it was supposed to end.

It was like listening to an old, scratchy vinyl record. The needle would be stuck in the grove, and you would have to lift the arm and move it to another part of the record. That's exactly how she felt—stuck in the same grove.

Her life had been full and complete; now it was empty and meaningless. Everyone had deserted her. Or so it seemed. Her own mother had said that she didn't understand her. Then, she never had.

Samara stared out the bedroom window in her grandmother's house. The ancient oak tree stood guard exactly as it had when she was a little girl. How many days had she tarried at that same window, talking to the old tree, making plans for the future? Nothing was going to stand in her way. She was going to be every woman—a career professional, a wife, and a mother. Now here she was, all grown up with nothing to show for her life but broken promises, a disjointed family, and weird, scary dreams.

"Where did I go wrong?" Samara demanded an answer from the loyal oak. "How can life start out so right and end up so messy?"

The old tree offered no response. Silent tears escaped down her face. Samara was so tired of crying. What she needed was answers. She slid off the bed and onto the new carpet. Lying on the floor was strangely comforting. It mirrored the sinking feeling she felt welling up inside her. She needed to get as close to the ground as she could. Rock bottom. This was it. No more free falls.

Her life had been perfect and tidy, everything in its place. That was then, and this was now. She had never been here before. It was a lonely, desperate place without her children. She needed them to know how much she loved them. They were the reason she dragged herself out the bed most mornings.

"Would they miss me if I were gone?" Samara pressed the silent oak for a response. "What if I just disappeared? Would anybody care?"

Her three children smiled back at her from the picture frame across the room. The photo had been taken the night before TJ died. They had gone to their favorite theme park that day. Tony had purchased a new camera and was taking pictures of everything within his view. He had begged them to pose just one more time. It turned out to be everyone's favorite shot. Life was good and they were happy. It seemed like an eternity ago.

Everyone had since moved on with their lives while she was forced to start over; It was as if she was the only one that couldn't get her act together. At least she was sure that her grandmother loved her. One day Samara would show her how much she appreciated everything that she had done. Right now, she could not reach past her own pain to express anything of real value. She wanted to hibernate under the covers for the next six months or until the pain wore off—whichever came first. Maybe then, she'd be okay.

Samara heaved the blanket from the bed, wrapping it around her tired body. The over-sized quilt smelled of her nana's favorite fabric softener. It felt good against her skin. She inhaled the fragrance, willing herself to relax. Sleeping on the floor would do the trick tonight. It just felt right.

For all it was worth, this was home for now. Only a select few knew where she was. Less is better. She needed the space to sort things out. Samara grabbed a pillow, stretched out on the carpet, pulled the blanket over her head, and was fast asleep within minutes.

Samara was dreaming, and she knew it. She wandered aimlessly through a meadow of exotic flowers, feeling dwarfed by the sheer magnitude of their height. There seemed to be neither beginning nor end to the strange garden. A kaleidoscope of indescribable colors adorned each blossomed array, like a gathering of royal peacocks. She basked in the splendor of the amazing experience.

An intoxicating aroma filled the air, reminding Samara of wild lavender and honeysuckle in the spring. The sun's rays seeped beneath the layers of her skin, filling her insides with tidal waves of peaceful calm. A smile of complete contentment spread across her face.

She came upon a young girl strolling leisurely several feet in front of her. The girl's long, curly tresses blew lazily in the gentle breeze. Samara saw her from behind, and it appeared the girl was reaching for her. The girl never looked back, but she had extended her arm behind her. Samara reached for the girl's hand. It was at first soft and comforting, but closed around her wrist like a steel vice. The girl turned toward Samara; her face had transfigured into a hideously grotesque mask.

Samara opened her mouth to scream, but the sound vanished before it reached the atmosphere. Nothing came out. The female creature had muted her voice. She struggled to get free, but the claw-like grip dug deeper into her wrists, drawing blood. The creature dragged Samara mercilessly through the field of flowers without ever looking back.

Where are you taking me? Samara pleaded telepathically with her captor.

"You've brought death to your Grandmother's house." The demon sneered. "She must die."

No!

What had she done to her beloved nana? This was all her fault.

"She will die, and you will watch."

They moved at superhuman speed. It seemed as if they were flying even though their feet never left the ground. Suddenly, a single building came into view. It stood alone in the middle of what appeared to be a vast wilderness. Samara recognized her grandmother's house.

* * *

Inside the house, Anna Morton awakened to a strange sound. She had fallen asleep in the den. It was her favorite place for prayer and devotion. The pain had been more intense than usual that night. She had not been able to walk to the stair glide. Samara must have covered her with the blanket before retiring.

Anna glanced over her shoulder, almost expecting to see someone—something. The pervading restlessness settled over the house. She sensed a presence that she could not decipher. The old house shifted on its foundation, whispering unheard secrets.

* * *

Outside, the demon drew closer to the house, taunting Samara with the impending death of her grandmother.

"Please," Samara begged, "let my Grandmother live. She's done nothing to deserve this."

"Your begging disgusts me." The demon mocked her. "Why should I let her live?"

"She's an innocent old woman. What harm can she be?"

They stopped directly outside of the house. The cuffs on Samara's wrist disappeared, sending her crashing face down on the ground.

"Beg for her life, you worthless coward!"

Samara gathered herself, staring directly in the face of her attacker. The dark angel seemed strangely familiar. Something in the hate-filled eyes resonated within her. When or where had she encountered this creature before?

The demon moved past Samara, making its descent into the house. She needed to save her grandmother.

"Nana!" she screamed.

* * *

Anna felt anxious, but was not strong enough to lift herself out of the chair. Her Bible lay open on the coffee table. She had been reading her favorite Psalm before drifting off, and thought it good to recite the verses aloud, as if to an unseen audience.

The LORD is my light and my salvation—whom shall I fear? The LORD is the stronghold of my life—of whom shall I be afraid? When evil men advance against me to devour my flesh, when my enemies and my foes attack me, they will stumble and fall. Though an army besiege me, my heart will not fear; though war break out against me, even then will I be confident. – Psalm 27: 1-3 (NIV)

She heard Samara cry out in her sleep. Max trotted into the den, yelping and wagging his tail. He sat by Anna, laying his head on her lap.

"I know Max." She buried her face in her weathered hands. "Father, help my grandbaby. Help us!"

* * *

Lariel moved from the den, piercing the walls to where Samara struggled in the throes of her dream. The brightness of his countenance receded. He would not confront the demon head on. His assignment must be carried out to the letter.

Thumar penetrated the house, appearing before Lariel.

"So we meet face-to-face, guardian." The dark angel leered.

Lariel kept silent. He had sensed the presence of the Deceiver's higher-ranking soldiers nearly 100 miles away. The demon was obviously unaware that he was merely a pawn.

"This one belongs to me," Thumar challenged Lariel.

"Then take her."

The dark angel bristled. Something was not right. Lariel's terrifying reputation preceded him. His legendary battle with Mastema was often discussed amongst Thumar's ranks. This was too easy. It was best to proceed with caution.

The human was aware that she was dreaming, but had not yet realized that he and Lariel were real. Thumar would see to it that she did not learn the truth. She must continue to believe that she is without help. He considered it a plus that Lariel had not yet revealed himself to her.

He chanced a quick glimpse of his sleeping victim. Lariel extended his wings, covering the human. Blinding light filled the room as he unsheathed his sword. It was a magnificent weapon. Thumar fell backwards. There was no way he was taking Lariel down by himself. It was not worth the risk.

There were others ready to join the revolt. It was time to gather his private battalion and destroy Lariel in the process. Thumar would go into hiding until he had determined his next move. He would have to re-engage his victim before she discovered the guardian.

"We'll meet again Lariel!" Thumar made a hasty exit.

"I'm counting on it."

Lariel drew closer to his sleeping subject and whispered in her ear. Satisfied that she would not be further disturbed, he returned to Anna and the dog. The elderly saint had fallen asleep praying. They were not alone. Her guardian had arrived while Lariel had tended to Thumar.

"Lariel, my brother." Jabniel greeted his fellow compatriot.

"I am grateful for the assistance." Lariel returned the salute.

"Gabriel has instructed us to engage the enemy together from this point."

"Were you able to estimate the number of enemy troops in the area?"

"They're small in number," Jabniel responded, "Clearly not a warring faction."

"That may change with their knowledge of your involvement."

"Thumar is playing a dangerous game. He's in over his head."

"We're not the ones he should be worried about." Lariel agreed. "Mastema has most likely given the order for his destruction."

Jabniel lifted the blanket from the floor and tucked Anna in securely.

"Sleep on dear one." Jabniel laid his finger on her temple. "Not much longer."

Lariel returned to his command post, where Gabriel awaited an update. Jabniel stayed behind.

I had a dream that made me afraid. As I was lying in my bed, the images and visions that passed through my mind terrified me.
—Daniel 4:5 (NIV)

Chapter Ix

Samara awakened to the smell of country bacon, fried potatoes, and homemade buttermilk biscuits. The aroma invaded her bedroom and tickled her nose. Another restless night had come and gone. She'd had another troubling dream.

Her grandmother's melodious voice drifted from the kitchen as she hummed along with the tune on the radio. Samara recognized the old hymn from her early years in church school. The teacher made them memorize every single verse.

At the time, Samara thought hymns were for boring, old people like her mother and stepfather. She and fellow classmates had made up other versions of the songs. They would pass around a piece of paper and scribble in their personal rendition whenever the teacher's back was turned. She must have had eyes in the back of her head because they were always caught. Those were the days, Samara mused.

The grandfather clock down the hall chimed eight choruses. It was time to face another day. She rolled on her back and closed her eyes. There was no particular reason to get up.

Hiding out under the blankets suited her just fine. Waking up to a new day simply meant dealing with more unanswered questions, and that was growing very old very fast. She had nothing to look forward to. As far as she was concerned, her best days were behind her.

She peeked from under the blanket. The earth was still spinning on its axis. Sunlight streaked in through the windows, blatantly defying her miserable disposition. Maximus lay stretched out on the carpet at the foot of the bed. It looked like he was still sleeping. Faithful Max. He was always there.

Mental snapshots of Tony and his new girlfriend floated through her mind, creating a churning sensation in the pit of her stomach. She wished she could stop the images, but they materialized without her permission. The happy couple probably never gave Samara a second thought, but *her* days were consumed with high definition still shots of them holding each other in passionate embraces.

"I can't take this," she whispered a desperate plea.

The sense of abandonment was ever present, but it didn't hurt as much when she slept. She would give anything for shorter days and longer nights. It was the only way to shut out the drowning noises of heartache and despair. The winter months were the best because it was dark by five. She could climb in bed early and will herself to sleep without feeling guilty. But even that was changing. Samara's issues were finding their ways into her nocturnal hiatuses.

She threw back the covers and confronted her day. The dream from the previous night lingered in the recesses of her mind. She remembered the promise: *An angel will go before you* … It was the last thing she had heard before waking up. The statement danced around her brain. If she could figure out why this was happening, maybe she could figure out how to deal with it.

There hadn't been much teaching done at her church on the subject of angels. In fact, it was almost never discussed. She was admittedly intrigued by the peculiar announcement. The idea of real angels purposely involving themselves with her life seemed a bit farfetched. She knew that the Bible says they exist and have specific assignments. But she was sure they had much more important things to do than show up in her dreams reciting cryptic messages.

As far as Samara was concerned, there was nothing in front of her that required a personal escort—nothing that warranted exclusive celestial involvement. If her past was any indication of what lay ahead, then her future looked dreadfully bleak.

She could have used their help when the bottom was falling out. It was too late for that now: no need to waste everybody's time. Whatever the meaning of the strange words, she was in no mood to spend her reserve energy trying to decipher the code. Her brain was already on overload.

Her thoughts turned toward her children. She had not heard from either Deb or Nicky in weeks. It wasn't right. Losing one child was heart wrenching enough. Not a day went by that she did not long for TJ. The absence of the two remaining children only intensified the pain. They were her lifeline. She was anxious to speak with them—to hear their voices. The feeling was apparently not a mutual one.

They had been so close. These days it just seemed easier for them to stay away. Samara wrung her hands in nervous reflection. It ate at her insides. She was just as much a victim, yet she could do nothing to make it better. Their lives had been so darned complicated. The best she could do was to allow them their space to wade through their process.

She stole what little comfort she could get by lurking on their Facebook pages. That was where they chose to express themselves without inhibition. At least they hadn't un-friended her, yet.

* * *

"Good morning sleeping beauty." Anna handed her granddaughter a mug of freshly percolated coffee with extra milk and sugar, just the way she liked it. "How's my baby girl?"

"Ok."

Samara cupped both hands around the mug, savoring the fragrance of the aromatic brew. She settled into her favorite seat at the kitchen table. Her grandmother had already started preparing supper. Breakfast was on the table.

"Sunday is the Lord's day," her nana had said on many occasions.

That meant all of the food was prepared ahead of time. They would eat midday supper right after church. It was always a feast. Samara loved watching her grandmother cook. She made it look so easy.

"I get the pleasure of your company for breakfast this morning?" Anna held her spatula midair.

"With all this cooking you've been doing, I figured I might as well oblige."

"You need to eat sweetheart."

"I know, Nana."

"Help yourself. Everything is nice and hot. I made all of your favorites." She turned back to the stove.

"You're too good to me. I feel so guilty."

"Why?"

"I feel like *I* should be cooking, cleaning, and doing laundry for *you*. It's the least I can do to carry my weight around here. You won't take any money from me. At least let me do something."

"You need your money more than I do." Anna turned to face her granddaughter. "You know your grandfather left me well taken care of. What else would I do if I couldn't cook or clean? I would be bored to tears. Now go ahead and eat something, child."

Samara plucked a homemade biscuit from the stack and began loading it with alternate layers of home fries, scrambled eggs, and bacon. For the final touch, she smothered the sandwich in buttery syrup. She was suddenly very hungry. It had been several days since she had eaten anything substantial.

"I've been having strange dreams." The unintended confession escaped Samara's lips in between bites.

"Strange, in what way?" Her Grandmother turned from her cooking.

"Like angels, and demons," Samara's voice dropped off, "And Tony."

"How do you know they're angels or demons?"

"I just know." Samara took another bite of the delicious concoction. "It's like I understand things that I normally wouldn't."

Anna flashed a curious look at her granddaughter. Last night she had heard Samara screaming in her sleep. She had been unable to check on her, because she'd had a rough night battling rheumatoid arthritis.

"What kind of things?" She pressed her granddaughter.

Samara polished off the last morsel, grabbed her coffee, and moved to the window that faced their backyard. Somebody was already bouncing a basketball that early in the morning. A car in desperate need of a new muffler rumbled down the driveway. Normal sounds for a Sunday morning, but Samara felt anything but normal.

There was no easy way to tell her grandmother about the dreams, but she had to try. Somebody needed to help her make sense of the nightmares. Either that or she would have to take matters into her own hands, whatever that meant.

"I can communicate with them without actually talking out loud." Samara turned from the window, searching her nana's face for any hint of disbelief.

"How's that possible?" It was Anna's turn to sit at the table.

"I'm not sure. It's all so weird."

"Where does Tony fit in all of this?"

"I don't really know." Samara returned to staring out the window.

The more she talked about the dreams, the more preposterous the whole thing sounded. She didn't want her grandmother to think that she had totally lost it. But maybe she had. Perhaps she was having a nervous breakdown. That was it. She never had one before, but she was certain that this must be what one felt like. Lord knows she had enough issues to justify the craziness.

Once again, Tony was at the core of her issues. He was always the lowest common denominator. Divorced three years and she was still paying for it. He, in the meantime, was off living the life fandango. If he needed some kind of help, like the dream implied, he'd never admit it. The man had walked away from his family because he could not live with the hand they had been dealt. Something inside of him snapped. TJ's death blindsided the whole family, but Tony never fully recovered.

Not to mention his secret little habit that he either could not or would not give up. Obviously, he would rather switch than fight. Samara wasn't trivializing his struggle. She had her own shortcomings to deal with, and Tony seemed too comfortable in his addiction. Was she supposed to don her superwoman outfit, go flying over there, and force him to change his ways?

Samara shook her head from side to side, as if answering an unheard question. She needed a savior of her own. *Let him save himself.*

"Maybe it's time you speak with someone." Her grandmother's voice summoned her back.

"Like who? I wouldn't feel comfortable telling just anybody."

"I'm sure my pastor wouldn't mind meeting with you." Anna gently prodded.

Samara wouldn't dream of hurting her nana's feelings, but pastoral guidance was the last thing she needed right now. That angle just didn't work for her. She had spent all of these years living what she thought was a good Christian life, and this is how she's rewarded?

Forget about finding comfort within the walls of the house of God. Members of her congregation had stopped speaking once they found out she and Tony had divorced. Those same folks that had visited their home and put their feet under her dining table had begun treating her as if she had some kind of deadly infectious disease. It was as if being in the same room with her made them more susceptible to contracting the dreaded "D" virus. God forbid they should be caught speaking with her in public. They would either pretend not to see her or would turn and walk in another direction.

"Bunch of phonies," she whispered through the screened window.

That's okay, she thought to herself. She would come up with a good reason to decline her nana's suggestion. *No sense wasting the good reverend's time.* Samara had never met him personally, but she could already imagine the "poor lost soul" expression on his face once she told her sob story. He'd probably go to pouring oil and everything. She might as well save her grandmother the embarrassment.

"I don't know, Nana." Samara tried to beg off. "He'll probably think I'm some kind of lunatic."

"Don't be silly. I'm sure he's heard it all."

"I doubt if he's heard *this*."

Samara moved back to the table and plopped down across from her grandmother. She watched the steam from the coffee pot swirl and evaporate into thin air—just like that creature in her dreams. A spine-chilling sensation coursed through her veins. The image of the dark angel loomed in her mind. Whatever or whoever it was, the intentions were clear. It wanted to destroy her, Tony, or both. The likelihood of experiencing more of the same kind of sleepless nights appeared inevitable.

Maybe she would visit her nana's pastor after all. What did she have to lose? If nothing else, the good reverend could at least confirm that she was losing her natural mind. It would be a good a place as any to start.

Her grandmother broke the reflective silence with the question that had been hanging between them since Samara arrived. She reached across the table and grabbed her granddaughter's hands.

"Do you still love him, Sweet Pea?"

Samara looked directly at her nana. She had asked herself the same thing at least a million times. It should be a no-brainer. By now, the answer should fall from her lips with relative ease. She should be shouting it from the rooftop:

Free at last, free at last. Thank God almighty …

No one sews a patch of unshrunk cloth on an old garment. If he does, the new piece will pull away from the old, making the tear worse.
—Mark 2:21 (NIV)

Chapter X

Noah Bromley stared in reverential awe at the new forty-six inch flat screen mounted on the wall. It was a thing of beauty. His members had recently presented the gift in appreciation of his serving for fifteen years as senior pastor of the Asbury Community Fellowship Church. They wanted to be sure that he was cutting edge.

The last television to grace the pastor's study was only nineteen inches and did not have cable, let alone Internet capabilities. It was so old that most of the colors blended together, turning everything and everybody on the screen a weird shade of greenish blue. Noah had only turned the thing on when the church was empty and too quiet.

This was unlike any electronic equipment he had ever owned. Everything else in the room seemed outdated by comparison. His laptop at home was nice, but this was a serious upgrade. His fingers skimmed lightly over the control pad. He could operate the TV using either his computer keyboard or his new android.

It had taken him several days to read all the instruction manuals. Familiarizing himself with the universal remote was enough to leave him scratching his head. There was but so much information his brain could handle in one sitting. He would be the first to admit that he was intimidated.

One of his tech-savvy parishioners had linked his stereo system to the computer. It was the icing on the cake, but the reception kept going out. He was forced to call in the troops to help get everything working properly.

"There you go, Reverend." The cable guy connected the last plug. "All done."

"I'm all set?" Noah could barely contain his excitement.

"You're good to go. Why don't you take it for a test drive?"

"Don't mind if I do."

"Just remember," the technician pointed to the buttons on the remote, "the red one turns everything on. This here is your toggle for when you want to switch between the TV and the computer. The rest is pretty self-explanatory."

"I'm sure it'll be a piece of cake once I get the hang of it."

Noah was ready for the nice man to leave so that he could be alone with his new toys. He didn't want to be rude, but his Saturday was getting away from him, and he still had his sermon to prepare. He had even hoped to sneak in a little college football before getting down to business.

"I wouldn't get too hung up on readin' that there owner's manual," the cable guy pointed to the open book on Noah's desk. "Those instructions are confusin' as all get out. Smart man like you will have it down in no time."

"I appreciate your confidence. I'll take all of that I can get."

"Glad to help. Oh, and I fixed the stereo connection too. Now you can play all your music through the iTunes app loaded on your computer. The sound will come through your big speakers. It'll be like the choir's singing right here in your office."

"Imagine that." Noah was itching to try it.

"Don't know who hooked this up before, but the wires weren't right. An amateur, I suspect."

"That was mighty kind of you."

"No problem, Reverend." The man flashed a toothy grin. "You can call me directly whenever you need some help. I figured it might score some extra points with the Big Guy. Maybe you can put in a good word for me?"

"I certainly will." Noah shook his hand.

"Thank you, Reverend. I'll let myself out."

Noah felt guilty for escorting the man out of his study so hastily with only a promise to pray. He could have at least suggested that he pray to the "Big Guy" himself. It was the perfect opportunity to discuss matters of the faith, but that would have taken up even more time.

Hopefully I'll have another chance, Noah thought.

He glanced at the Bible concordance lying open on the desk. His father had given it to him when he graduated from seminary. The leather-bound, cross-referenced edition had been passed down ceremoniously through three generations of Bromleys. Its worn edges gave testament to the faithfulness of its previous owners. Scribbled notes, none of which belonged to

Noah, crammed the margins. He preferred to do his research on the Internet, and generally spent hours surfing the web for sermon ideas.

Noah grabbed the remote control, toying with the idea of actually turning the television on. He had much rather watch the games on the forty-six inch, high definition, screen-on-screen wonder. He could channel surf until he was cross-eyed. That was his idea of a Saturday afternoon well spent. Running a church was not. He had his parents to thank for that.

Ever since Noah could remember, his future vocation had been rehearsed repeatedly, until he knew nothing else. Noah would be a pastor; just like his father, grandfather, and great-grandfather before him. His family was not about to let him break with tradition. The matter was settled and was not open for discussion or debate.

Noah's life had been that of a textbook "preacher's kid." When his friends were out playing and doing what kids normally do, he was at the church cleaning the bathrooms, vacuuming the carpet, or scraping gum from underneath the pews. When he was older, he worked in the church office. His father made sure that he learned every aspect of running a church.

"Pastoring a church is more than just preaching a sermon, son." Noah could still hear his father's admonition. "If you're not fit to scrub toilets, then you're not fit to shepherd the flock."

Noah loved his father. He just did not have the same sentiments that many of his parishioners had. His father was a man's man, for certain, and had taken good care of his family. He had been a man of integrity, with high moral standards.

Even so, Noah never had the benefit of a normal relationship with his dad. The church always came first, at the expense of the family. It was the price you paid for being a "PK."

"Your father's not the kind to show his emotions outwardly," his mother had said, "But he loves you deeply."

Noah didn't buy it. That deep love his mother talked about was rarely expressed toward him, not in ways that Noah was able to quantify. Instead, his father's affections were given without measure to the members of his beloved church. It was never too early or too late for a troubled member to call the house. The phone rang at all hours of the day and night.

Noah spent many hours alone at the parsonage while his parents hurried off to comfort a member whose loved one had died or to pray with some distraught soul. It was during those moments that he wished he had never been born a pastor's son. He despised the discipline that his father imposed on his life. Responsibility and commitment took precedence over having fun.

Noah had been away at seminary, finishing his last year, when he had learned of his father's illness. Someone from student affairs came to his classroom and handed the professor a note. To this day, Noah still could not figure out how he knew the note was for him. A reverential hush swept over the classroom as the professor asked Noah to step outside to the hallway.

"I'm very sorry," the professor could scarcely hide the profound sadness in his eyes, "but your father has taken ill quite suddenly. Your mother has asked that you call home immediately."

He did not cry at his father's funeral. The old man would not have wanted him to appear weak or unglued in public. Never let them see you sweat. His father had always been in control of his emotions. Noah was to represent the family in that same honorable Bromley fashion. He held his mother's hand during the entire service, wondering what life would be like without his dad.

For many years, he had convinced himself that he resented his father. Sitting in front of the church, he finally understood what his mother had tried telling him all along. His father had loved him deeply and had expressed it the only way he knew. Now he was gone.

Noah looked around the study, remembering how it had been when his father was the pastor. Little had changed. Not even the furniture. The antique desk still held some of his father's knick-knacks in the little cubbyholes. He could almost smell the old man's cologne. The room had seemed larger then. Maybe it had been his father's larger-than-life presence.

What he would not give for a normal life. He wanted the nine-to-five, the wife and kids, and maybe a pet of some kind. He had promised himself that he would have it. His family would come first, and they would know how much he loved them.

Noah pushed back from the desk, stretching his lanky six foot two inch frame. He stole a quick glance at himself in the tall dressing mirror.

Not bad, he sized himself up, *considering you're almost an old man.*

He took extra care to stay in shape, just as his father had taught him. One of the guestrooms in the small parish doubled as his workout area. He kept a strict physical regimen, spending at least one hour a day on the machines. His biological clock was ticking louder these days. At forty-something, he was growing more anxious about his appearance. With every celebrated birthday, hopes of meeting Ms. Right slipped further into darkness.

He thought he had found true love several years back. However, his hopes for making her the new Mrs. Bromley were shattered the day he popped the question. The object of his affection ran for the hills. Said she was not ready to be a pastor's wife, let alone a mother.

She begged him to try to see it from her perspective. Her career was finally kicking into high gear after having grunted it out and sucked it up for ten long years. Marrying a pastor would bring all of her hard-earned accomplishments to a screeching halt. She loved him, but could not see devoting her precious time to his church with all those "needy members." Couldn't they just "be together"?

After that fiasco, Noah dated every single woman within a hundred mile radius, or so it seemed. There was always sister so-and-so's friend of a friend—who knows this girl. Even the ladies in the Seasoned Saints Club got in on the search. He soon grew weary of the blind dates and awkward encounters, and began politely declining invitations. The pursuit for the perfect wife ended. He'd had enough.

His friends gave up on him too. They told him he was on his own. Maybe he *was* being a little too picky, but he reserved that right. "Till death do us part" is a long time. He had performed enough extravagant weddings to know that what he wanted was the woman who would hang around for the marriage.

He buried himself in church work. There was always plenty of that to go around.

"An idle mind is the devil's workshop," his father had rehearsed with him more times than he could remember.

Maybe the old man was right, Noah thought. Keeping busy was the best weapon against the ever-present reminders that he was still without a mate. Throwing himself into his work left little time for obsessing over the pain of having no one to love. Besides, he wasn't so sure he would even recognize that "special someone" if she walked up and bit him.

Noah wandered over to the window and stared longingly at the outdoors. His heart yearned to be somewhere else. Admiring the wondrous display of God's handiwork was one of Noah's favorite things to do. It was a beautiful autumn morning. The leaves were just beginning to turn colors, creating a postcard-like splendor of yellows, oranges, and reds.

He rubbed the back of his clean-shaven head. Here he was, spending another Saturday searching for something more satisfying. He longed to experience that *joie de vivre,* that joy of living that seemed just out of his reach. He loved God and was secure in his relationship with Him, but this emptiness called for something that would only be filled by another someone.

However, this was not the time for self-loathing or pity. Noah returned to his sermon notes. His faithful parishioners would be expecting to hear a well-prepared message, something that mattered. They deserved at least that much. He needed to come up with something they had not already heard a thousand times before. The Bromley tradition must continue.

"Pastor?" Barbara Johnson, the church secretary, knocked softly, poking her head through the door.

"Yes?" Noah withdrew from his bewildered state.

"There's someone here to see you."

He didn't recall scheduling anyone other than the cable guy. Saturday's were short enough as it was. He was not interested in spending the last of his precious moments listening to someone go on and on about something they had no intention of changing.

"Do they have an appointment?"

"No."

It was all she said, but she didn't have to say any more. Barbara had been the church secretary for more than twenty-five years. She was there when Noah was only a teen. No one questioned her loyalty to the pastor or to the church. The discreet assistant knew far more than her genteel manner ever revealed. *MASH* had Radar, Asbury had Barbara Johnson. Noah reckoned her his mother from another other. She was his second mom.

"Who is it?" He trusted her judgment.

"Samara Daniels." A mischievous smile danced across the secretary's face and disappeared just as quickly. "She's the granddaughter of Anna Morton."

"Is Mrs. Morton okay?"

"Oh, she's fine." Barbara was obviously not going to say why she was granting Samara Daniels special passage.

"Give me five minutes, and then send her in."

"Of course." She closed the door behind her.

When a strong man, fully armed, guards his
own house, his possessions are safe.
—Luke 11:21 (NIV)

Chapter XI

THE HOUSE APPEARED EMPTY. He had spied out the neighborhood before entering through the basement. The massive trees had provided ample cover. As far as he could tell, no one followed him.

Thumar moved through the unsettling darkness, tossing an occasional glance over his shoulder. He must not draw any unwanted attention. There was no movement but his. No one was home but the stupid dog, and yet ... Every room vibrated with electrified energy. His nondescript form absorbed the night, but the darkness provided little protection. An uneasy quiet permeated the house.

It seemed as if the unoccupied residence had a life of its own. He felt the foundation shift, as if the old house knew he was trespassing. As if it would spit him out, exposing him. He must move quickly.

Thumar was not sure what he was looking for, but he would know when he found it. There had to be something in the house that explained the recent events. The atmospheres crackled with curious activity, and this human was at the center. Mastema's unprecedented involvement only gave further credibility to the rumors. Something peculiar was underfoot.

He penetrated the ceilings, arriving on the second floor landing. Everything in him screamed, "Leave this place!" but he had determined to up the ante. The playing field was about to be leveled. He needed hard-core evidence to take back to his newly formed contingent. It had to be something stronger than a hunch, if the others were to defect to his side.

Thumar would no longer rely on the meager bits of intel sifted through the rank and file. The risk factor was too high. His hide was on the line, and he intended to save it. The way he saw it, he had the upper hand. He had studied the girl for years. Mastema wasn't the only one with a stake in the spineless human. No one else had been appointed to her. This human was his ticket to the inner circle. She was his alone.

He perused the second floor hallway, stopping short of the girl's bedroom. Thumar hesitated. Something was wrong. The dog was sitting at the top of the landing, almost as if standing guard. He knew the animal sensed his presence. The hairs on its back were raised and it was barking. Thumar could easily handle the dog. That was not it.

An unidentifiable force prohibited his access. The exterior of the girl's room was impenetrable. He could not go any further. That blasted Lariel! The guardian was most likely observing from a distance. He would love nothing more than to lure Thumar into a trap. One slip and Thumar was as good as dead—or worse.

He backed away, releasing a string of obscenities into the atmosphere. He pierced through the hallway into the grandmother's bedroom. Perhaps he would find something useful in the old woman's possession.

A silhouette shifted in the night.

"What took you so long?" Putnah's beady eyes glared through the shadows.

"Why are you here?" Thumar hissed at sniveling demon. "Who sent you?"

"Zarian. My orders were to wait for you here."

"I'm fully capable of overseeing my own mission. Zarian was not to do anything until I instructed him."

"I was to warn you of possible enemy activity."

"And?"

"I'm not sure, but it doesn't seem like we're alone."

"Did you see anything?"

"Only the animal." Putnah looked about nervously. "Still, something doesn't seem right. I don't think we should stay here much longer. The word is out. Mastema has given the order to have you trailed."

"Where did you hear that?" Thumar was visibly shaken.

"From a loyal comrade. It's very likely we're being watched right now."

"Why should I believe you? You didn't see anything."

"Mastema doesn't trust you." Putnah bristled in the darkness. "That's enough reason."

Thumar rubbed the scar on his face. If Mastema were to get wind of his plans, he would be destroyed. He must be more careful. Only those with demonstrated loyalty would be trusted. This did not include Putnah. The little demon was too squirmy.

Thumar had a plan. He would set up shop and execute his own covert operation. A nearby church had proven to be the ideal hideout for his new converts. The congregation had ceased being a threat to the kingdom of darkness years before. The pastor no longer referred to the Bible as the final authority. Instead, he lulled the humans to sleep by telling jokes and referencing popular psychologists and new age philosophers.

The shift was so subtle most of the humans did not even notice. Those that dared complain were made to feel so uncomfortable that they eventually left; taking with them the angelic hosts that covered the church. There was nothing to keep out the likes of Thumar and his cohorts. He did not anticipate any interference from the enemy's camp.

He did not have much time before he was to report to Mastema, and he did not intend to being humiliated ever again. The next time they met, Thumar would be the one giving the orders.

It would not be easy, but everyone had a chink in their armor—even Mastema. Thumar figured it to be Lariel. If he could find a way to bait the guardian, the rest would fall into place.

* * *

Lariel and his comrade, Jabniel, watched from their command post at a nearby house. The homeowners had formed a neighborhood prayer group, and had unknowingly provided adequate cover for the angelic hosts.

The guardians looked toward the sky. It was darker than usual. Mastema's contingent was keeping close tabs on Thumar. They had trailed Putnah, the nervous little demon, to the house.

Thumar was clearly taking matters into his own hands. The demon had enlisted the aid of fellow malcontents. Neither Lariel nor Jabniel would interfere. Their orders were to allow the events to unfold. The enemy would have limited access to the girl and her grandmother—for now.

You have stolen my heart, my sister, my bride; you have stolen my heart with one glance of your eyes, with one jewel of your necklace.
—*Song of Solomon 4:9 (NIV)*

Chapter XII

Samara Daniels stood before him, a contradiction of statements. She was quite lovely in a disarming kind of way— breathtaking, really. Yet her demeanor suggested gentility uncommon in most women he would consider beautiful. It was as if she didn't realize the extent of her own attractiveness.

The brisk October air had flushed her cheeks. She wore very little make up and did not appear to need any more than that. Her shoulder length hair cascaded into soft, brown ringlets, framing a perfectly oval-shaped face. The deep-set hazel eyes sparkled with flecks of green and gold. They seemed to look right through him.

Noah figured her to be about five foot five in the low-heeled ankle boots. Coordinated accessories complimented a stylish sweater dress that seemed tailored for her frame. A paisley patterned shawl casually draped her shoulders. In her hands, she clutched a small suede purse. He recognized the designer's insignia on the clasp.

Everything matched flawlessly, yet nothing was overdone. She was a picture of understated elegance. He could not take his eyes off her.

"Thank you for seeing me on such short notice, Reverend Bromley." Samara extended her hand.

Electric waves coursed through Noah's arm the moment her hand touched his. They caught him totally off guard. He had never experienced anything like them. His heart raced as he wondered if Samara had noticed his reaction, but she did not appear affected either way. She remained where she stood, looking slightly embarrassed as she waited for him to release her hand. He had not realized that he was still holding it.

"Certainly." Noah's voice cracked as he reluctantly gave her hand back. "Please have a seat."

Get it together, Noah. This isn't like you. You are a grown man, for goodness sake. She's just another woman with a problem.

"How is your grandmother faring these days?" He deferred to his proper upbringing and ministerial decorum. "I'm afraid I haven't been very good about getting over to see her."

"She sends her love." Samara's smile revealed the slightest hint of a dimple on one side of her face.

The fragrance of her perfume drifted across the desk as she settled into the visitor's chair. It was subtle, yet alluring. He recognized the scent but could not place it. Whatever it was, it was now his favorite.

Noah stole a quick glance at her ring finger and was relieved to see nothing on it. His brain told him to slow down, but the rest of him was on automatic pilot.

"Your grandmother is one of our most faithful members." He forced his attention back to the conversation. "I know when she's not feeling well. It's the only time she's not here on a Sunday."

"That's my nana." Samara's smile broadened. "It has to be pretty bad for her not to come."

"I don't recall ever seeing you with her in church."

Noah hoped that had not sounded condemning. He wanted her to feel comfortable.

"No, well … Nothing personal, Reverend, but Asbury was never really my cup of tea." She offered an apologetic glance. "No offense."

I totally get it, beautiful lady. You would be surprised.

"None taken." Noah raised his hands in a surrendering gesture. "There are enough churches around here to suit everyone's taste. So what brings you this way today?"

Her charming disposition captivated him. She was clearly troubled about something, yet she exhibited great poise. It seemed to be a true representation of her character. This was not a performance. In many ways, she was very much like her grandmother. The similarities were remarkable.

"I don't know where to begin." She released a nervous giggle. "Now that I'm here I feel kind of silly."

The pleasure's all mine, Noah thought.

"Don't be bashful. Jump right in." He reclined in his chair in an effort to exhibit a modicum of self-control.

"Well, the past few years have been quite challenging, to say the least. A lot of things have happened; too much to talk about, really." She picked idly at a loose piece of thread on the armrest. "I guess you can say that everything that could have gone wrong, did. When it was all said and done, I ended up moving in with my grandmother."

"I'm sure you're a big help to her around the house." Noah offered.

"Oh, she's no slouch. She's got more energy than I do when she's feeling okay. But the reason for my visit isn't really my grandmother."

Noah nodded his head. The story sounded like it was going to be good. He would let her do the talking. The reason for her being there did not much matter to him. He would be content to sit and watch her do absolutely anything.

"Take all the time you need." He encouraged Samara to continue. "I can have my secretary fix something warm to drink; a cup of tea perhaps?"

"I wouldn't want to be a bother."

"No bother at all. Knowing her, she's probably already heating up the water."

"Thank you, but I don't want to take up too much of your time." She entwined the thread around her index finger. "There's no way to say this without sounding a little loony, so I'll get right to the point."

Samara fidgeted ever so slightly. She was still smiling, but her eyes whispered a deep sadness. There was more to the woman than her outward appearance would suggest. Haunting secrets lay beneath that beautiful exterior, and Noah aimed to find out what they were.

"I've been having these weird dreams lately," she continued. "They started several months back, right before I moved in with

Nana. At first, I thought they were your textbook nightmares, but then I kept having them. The weird part is that they seem to have some kind of common theme—as if they're all connected somehow."

Noah remained in his reclined position. He hadn't heard anything worth being worked up over. Everyone has the occasional nightmare, but this was her show. He would give her time to get to the real purpose of the visit.

"Can you think of anything that might be causing these nightmares?" He did not want to appear unconcerned. "Maybe you're eating too close to bedtime?"

"I doubt if this has anything to do with my diet." A sarcastic smirk replaced the beautiful smile.

Great, Noah—why don't you just insult the lady to her face with your corny clergy humor?

"Now it's my turn to offer an apology." Noah blushed. "I didn't mean to trivialize your situation. It must be quite disturbing for you to seek help."

"It is, or I wouldn't be here." She looked him straight in the eyes.

"Again, my apologies. Please continue."

"Well," she hesitated, "the reoccurring messages seem to have something to do with these other-worldly beings."

"Can you be a little more specific?"

"Yes. Well, like angels and demons." She stumbled over the words. "They seem to want something from me."

"Please don't take this as an insult or anything," Noah sat upright in his chair, "but what makes you think what you're seeing are angels and demons?"

"That's the million dollar question. I am able to understand things without really thinking about it. It's like having a steady stream of information downloaded into my brain all at once."

"Sounds pretty intense." Noah was intrigued. "Do these beings identify themselves?"

"Yes and no." Her eyes pleaded with him. "As soon as I come into contact with them I already know who they are. Or, I guess I should say that I know what they are. They seem to know me very well. I can tell by the things they say. When they communicate, it's telepathically. But I hear the words just as if they had spoken them out loud."

"You said that they seem to want something from you. Do you have any idea what that might be?"

Samara's eyes instantly filled with tears that flowed effortlessly down her face. Noah reached for the tissues that Barbara kept stocked in his desk for just such occasions. After years of counseling, he knew the drill. They were about to get to the crux of the matter. He would remain silent and allow her time to gather herself.

"I'm sorry." Samara dabbed her eyes with the offered tissues. "I know how odd this must sound. The more I repeat it, the more ridiculous I feel. I keep telling myself that it's nothing more than symptoms of stress and fatigue, but I cannot shake this sense of urgency. I've even started praying again in hopes of getting some kind of clarity."

"Has that helped?" Noah was happy for the first bit of normalcy.

"I really can't say. The more I pray, the more I feel as if I were supposed to be doing something. But for the life of me, I just can't figure out what that something is." Samara blew her nose quietly. "It's totally frustrating. Nana believes that God still speaks through dreams, and she is convinced that this is all happening for a reason. She thought that talking with you might help give me some direction."

Noah clasped his hands and whispered a silent prayer. He didn't know where to begin with this one. The Bible was clear on the existence of angels and demons, but he had never counseled anyone that claimed to have had direct interaction. When he was in school, he had studied the subject of dreams and interpretations. It raised more questions than answers.

From what he could tell, the woman sitting on the other side of his desk was of sound mind and body—especially body. He had no reason to believe that she had somehow taken leave of her senses. This seemingly well-adjusted, intelligent person had apparently experienced something very disturbing.

"I think your grandmother gave you good advice." Noah looked directly into the tear-filled eyes. "There's no need to suffer in silence. Don't you worry about how it sounds. Believe me; you get to hear it all after twenty years of counseling. We will get to the bottom of this. I'll call around to some of my pastor friends too. This probably isn't as strange as you think."

"Thank you so much pastor." Samara looked somewhat relieved for the first time. "I'm sure that you have a lot more important things to do than to figure out some crazy lady's weird dreams."

A fleeting smile crossed her face as she tenderly touched the beautiful gold chain resting around her neck. Noah noticed the charm dangling at the end of the necklace. On it were several birthstones surrounding the word *Mom*. He hadn't once considered that this woman was somebody's mother.

"Everybody's important at Asbury." Noah smiled. "We are all family here. And, no worries; everything will be held in the strictest of confidence."

He wanted to prolong their visit. The new television no longer mattered.

"Are you sure I can't get you that cup of tea?" He offered.

"No, thank you." Samara stood, gathering the scarf around her shoulders. "I must be going. Nana is alone in the house."

"Of course," Noah prepared to escort her out. "Please let your grandmother know that I am praying for her."

"I will." Samara hesitated at the door. "Do you think she's right about God speaking to regular people through dreams?"

"Anything's possible." Noah guarded his response. "He is God after all. Let me do a little research on the subject."

"Thank you, Reverend."

Okay, Noah, you may never see this woman face-to-face again. It's now or never. Speak up, man!

Noah cleared his throat.

"Well there's no need to stand on formality, is there? Please call me Noah."

"Okay, as long as you don't call me crazy." She giggled.

"I promise." He returned the smile. "Would it be okay if I give you a call after I've done my research? Perhaps we can meet over coffee?"

"I'd appreciate that." Samara extended her hand once again. "I'll leave the number with the secretary?"

"That works." Noah shook her hand and returned it promptly. "I have one of those new Android phones and haven't figured out how to add contacts. I should grab one of the kids in Sunday school tomorrow. They can probably program the thing with their eyes closed."

"Isn't it crazy? It's their world." She opened the door. "Good night, Reverend—Noah."

"Good night, Samara. I'll talk to you soon."

The secretary was busy putting the final touches on Sunday's church bulletin when the door opened. Her desk faced the main entrance to the outer office, so her back was to Noah and Samara. Neither of them saw the smile spreading across the elderly woman's face.

"Ms. Johnson." Noah walked up behind her. "Please take down Ms. Daniel's number."

"Of course, Reverend."

For although they knew God, they neither glorified him as God, nor gave thanks to him, but their thinking became futile and their foolish hearts were darkened.
—*Romans 1:21 (NIV)*

Chapter XIII

Matthew Donaldson rinsed each plate carefully before stacking them in the dishwasher. It was his week for kitchen duty. The house chores were posted in a prominent place, and he was not about to let anyone accuse him of shirking his responsibilities. He was no freeloader.

Someone in the living room yelled at the ESPN sportscaster. Matt chuckled as he scraped the remains from the last pot and switched on the garbage disposal. The guys were psyched about the big game. After church, they would all change into sweatshirts and caps displaying their team's logo. It made for a rowdy afternoon. Matt would just as soon stay in his room and surf the net. He was not a big sports enthusiast, not compared to most, anyway.

Still, he was lucky to land in this particular group home. The previous recovery facility had been too close to his old stomping grounds. Some of the same guys were still hanging around just as they had when he had left for the military. Their game was as tired as the lies they told. Nothing had changed.

The old crew was determined to pull Matt right back in. But he had seen more than his share of trouble. They had nothing he wanted. The waiting list for the New Life group home had been long, but his social worker had never given up. Matt had moved away from the old facility as soon as a room at New Life had become available.

Matt turned the dishwasher knob and pushed it in. The old appliance hummed in obedience as the water splashed about. He opened the back door and shook out the rug just as the van was pulling up to the curb. It would carry the men to Asbury Community Fellowship Church for Sunday service. If you chose to be a resident at New Life, then you agreed to honor the principles: respect, responsibility, and religion. That was their credo. Church attendance was mandatory. Everyone was required to attend regular service, and then again on Wednesday nights for Bible study. Anybody that did not get with the program got transferred.

"Hey." It was Eric, the house captain. "I wanted to talk to you real quick before everybody comes down."

"What's up?" Matt wiped his hands on the dishtowel.

"Nothing bad. It's all good actually." Eric leaned against the entranceway. "The director and I were talking, and we think you might be ready for the group leader spot. With Doug leaving next week, we're going to need someone to fill in."

Matt folded the towel and placed it on the rack. He wanted to take his time answering. This would be a big step in his recovery process—one he was not so sure he was ready to take. He had already sacrificed years of his life following a course that someone else had charted. The price was more than he had been willing to pay. But that was then, and this was now. He had nothing to prove anymore.

"I'm not sure I can handle that kind of responsibility right now." He told his house captain. "Those are some pretty big shoes to fill. Doug knows these guys. They respect him."

"And they'll respect you too, in time." Eric assured him.

"I like minding my own business. It keeps me out of trouble."

"Listen Matt, I hear what you're saying. I really do. However, you have shown tremendous growth since coming here two years ago, and we really believe you have the potential to be a great leader. Trust me; I would not be approaching you if everybody didn't feel good about it. You can handle this. And you won't be doing it alone."

"Let me think about it. Do you need an answer right now?"

"No. Take your time." Eric patted him on his shoulder. "Like I said, Doug is here until next week, so mull it over. Let me know by Saturday though. We have a backup plan, but we're hoping not to use it."

"Okay." Matt extended his hand. "Thanks man. I appreciate your confidence in me."

"No problem." Eric shook his hand. "You about finished up in here?"

"Yep. Just need to get my tie." Matt grabbed the dishcloth and wiped down the table.

"Get the other guys together. We don't want to go strolling into the church late, like last week."

"That wouldn't be cool. You are looking at the newest member of parking lot security. I'm going to need to be there early from now on."

"Parking security?" Eric kidded. "We're coming up in the world."

"Pastor caught me after service last week and asked if I'd consider helping out. No one was surprised as I was." Matt confessed. "I told him I was with New Life."

"What did he say to that?"

"He said that they could use some new life around there."

"Imagine that. I guess we're not the only ones who want to see you move forward. While we're at it, I think it's a good time for you to start leading morning prayer."

Matt knew it was coming. Group leaders inherited the duty of calling everyone together for prayer. This was a testing-the-waters kind of thing.

"I think it'll be a good way to prepare the others for the change. That is, if you take us up on our offer. You okay with that?"

"It's cool."

"You sure?"

"I'm sure."

"Okay." Eric fixed his eyes on Matt. "Tell me if you think it's too much. That is not what we are about here. And don't forget to let me know your final decision about the group leader thing by Saturday."

Matt climbed the three flights that led from the kitchen to his room. The big house had two sets of stairs—one in the front of the house and the other in the back. It was an old house in the Cobbs Creek section of the city.

When he had first arrived, he had had to share a room with another group member. It was the only time he'd had an altercation. Matt had proven he could take care of himself. No one had bothered him since. After two years of staying out of trouble and following the rules, he had earned the position of group leader. He had come a long way since his days of being on the streets.

He had spent the majority of his young life hanging with the wrong crowd, which often landed him in juvy. It kept him moving from one facility to another. They were not the kinds of places where good things generally happen.

A truant officer at one of the detention centers had taken a special interest in Matt, and had suggested he enlist in the military. He said he would rather see Matt die for a noble cause than in the streets. The counselors had seen their shares of tragedy from lives ended too soon. If Matt had continued down the road that he had been travelling, he would have been sure to end up the same.

Joining the military had proven to be a welcomed change. Matt had selected the field of technology as a joke, not believing he would do well enough to pass the test. Heck, he had thought the guy at the recruiting station would laugh him right of the office. To Matt's surprise, he not only passed the test but also scored in the top percentile. He still believed his test scores were mixed up with somebody else's. Some poor slug had probably ended up working in the mess hall.

He had finally found the thing that satisfied his inner longings. Turned out, he was good with computers. Using state of the art technology while having access to top level military information exposed him to a world he had not known existed. He had loved it. Taking things apart and figuring out how to fix things were the coolest things he had ever done.

For the first time that Matt could remember, his family had shown pride in him. They had attended his basic training graduation en mass—everyone but his dad. No one was surprised.

After his military discharge, he'd had a difficult time finding employment. The technology field had been shrinking fast. Jobs were scarce, with many positions outsourced to other countries. Oddly enough, there were very few jobs for military veterans.

His mother had always said that misery loves company. She must have been right, because he eventually returned to the same self-destructive patterns. He was back on the streets. This time he was introduced to the latest drug. It would cost him ten years of his life. He did things he never imagined he would do to support his habit.

He ended up in the municipal courthouse. The judge was lenient because Matt was ex-military. He was given two options. Either he entered a faith-based rehabilitation program, or he went to jail. He chose the program.

The home was a crucial part of Matt's recovery. It was the last phase of rehabilitation before re-entering society. There was no looking back.

"The van is here!" Matt called out at the top of the second landing, "Time for prayer."

Dante, the youngest resident was still in the bathroom, singing at the top of his voice. He was always the last one ready.

"I'm coming!" He sang out.

"Five minutes dude." Matt knocked on the bathroom door.

Dante opened the door and stepped into the hallway like a runway model at a photo shoot. A steamy collage of shaving lotion and mouthwash aromas floated from the bathroom. He was in full regalia.

"Man, you know I got to look right!" Dante took to the catwalk like a pro.

"You've had all morning."

"You can't rush perfection, Mister No Style."

"I guess that depends on what you might call perfect."

"Not like you'd know the difference." Dante strutted off towards his room.

Matt shook his head. For a guy that wasn't all that crazy about church, Dante sure took getting ready rather seriously. Everything had to be just so. He had said that he never knew where he might meet his future wife.

That was fine for Dante, but Matt was not interested in meeting anybody right now, and especially not in the church. No Christian woman in her right mind would want anything to do with the likes of someone like him.

He was trying to get his own life together. Dealing with relationship drama was not on his list of things to do. Besides, it would take someone special to accept him for who he was—a recovering addict.

My prayer is not that you take them out of the world
but that you protect them from the evil one.
—*John 17:15 (NIV)*

CHAPTER XIV

SAMARA WALKED PURPOSEFULLY DOWN the school corridor. The long, narrow hallway stretched for miles. She was late for class again, and the heavy backpack was slowing her down. This time, there would be trouble. Her homework was not done. Neither could she remember the room number. The teacher had already warned her about coming to class tardy and unprepared.

She peeked through each door hoping to spot a familiar face, but found none. All the rooms were empty. The chairs were upside down on the desks. It seemed she was alone in the maze-like building. The clicking of her heels against the concrete floor ricocheted off the walls as she hurried on. Her echoing footsteps were the only sounds heard.

Samara veered left at the end of the hall and headed for the stairs leading to the second floor. As she began her ascent, the backpack instantly morphed into a casket. She knew without looking that she was carrying her father. The casket weighed almost as much as she did.

The heavy sarcophagus thumped against the stairs behind her as she climbed to the next landing. She stopped on the third floor and adjusted the shoulder straps. Lugging her father on her back was a small price to pay. At least he was with her.

By the time she reached the fourth floor, she felt the coffin had decreased in size and was easier to manage. That was when she saw her teacher waiting in the hallway with her arms crossed in front of her. Samara entered the room and placed the backpack-sized casket on her desk. Her teacher followed close behind, displaying exaggerated annoyance. It didn't matter; Samara's dad would protect her.

"Why are you late?" The teacher pointed an unusually long ruler dangerously close to Samara's face.

"I'm sorry." Samara took a step backward. "It wasn't my fault. I couldn't find the room."

"That is unacceptable!" The teacher slammed the ruler on Samara's desk. "The rest of your classmates should not have to suffer just because you can't seem to get your little life together. Hold out your hands!"

Samara stepped even farther away from the irate teacher. She would not let her hurt her again.

"I said, hold your hands out!"

A hissing sound slithered from the teacher's mouth. Her face transfigured into a visage of pure evil. Samara instantly recognized the dark angel. The hate-filled eyes leered back at her. They had met again, but this time she knew him.

"Destroy her!" Thumar ordered.

The demons circled Samara, taunting her with threatening gestures and lewd remarks. Their slime-infested bodies slammed against her mercilessly. Gristly, claw-like appendages clawed the air. They struck Samara repeatedly, knocking her to the floor.

"Where's your father now?" They mocked.

Samara threw herself on the backpack, using her body as a shield. She shut her eyes against the attack. It did not matter what they did to her, they would not take her father away again.

At that moment, a thought came to her. She heard it above the noise of her assailants, even though it was spoken quietly within.

Pray, the voice said.

She whispered the only thing she knew.

"Lord, save me."

The room grew suddenly still. Samara dared not open her eyes. She didn't know what was happening. A peaceful silence had replaced the jeering and taunting. Something had changed. She could feel that she was no longer encircled. The evil presence was gone.

Samara. It was the same voice.

She slowly opened her eyes. There stood before her the most beautiful thing she had ever seen. Resplendent light draped the winged creature's bronze form. Its massive body electrified the room. An indescribable translucence lay just beneath the jeweled armor. The handle of a magnificently crafted sword protruded from the golden sheath. It looked at least ten feet long.

Samara was looking into the eyes of an angel. She understood without explanation that this glorious being was there to protect her. The understanding of this truth released a joy within that she had never imagined possible. Someone was really looking out for her.

Lariel spread his wings in a cocooning fashion. He would transport her from this state of unconsciousness. She needed to get back without another interruption. He held her gaze.

"You are never alone." The guardian said.

"Daddy!" Samara cried out in her sleep.

She woke up crying. Whether because of the vision, or the unrequited longing for her father, she wasn't sure. She had come face-to-face with the sadness she had been lugging around all these years.

Samara's father had died before she was born. She had gleaned what little she knew about him from her grandmother. Seems he had been quite the ladies' man, or so she was told. Her mother rarely spoke of him. Whenever Samara would ask questions, her mother answered in as few words as possible.

The only picture of her father that she was aware of was the one on the mantle in her grandmother's living room. It was taken the day he graduated from basic training. He looked so handsome in his military uniform, and so young. The smile on his face spoke of a life filled with good things to come. But there would be no more pictures. He never made it back from Vietnam.

Nana said that it was the reason her mother had moved away. Her mother had wanted a better life for the both of them, but that had meant she would have to leave Samara. Tears had streamed down both their faces as she had explained why it had to be that way. She had promised Samara that it was for the best, and that she would never let anyone mistreat her.

Samara was four when she was taken to Delaware to live with the Carlton family. It was the first of many foster homes. They weren't really foster homes per se. Back then, folks took in children to make extra money. Samara's mother knew the Carlton's well, and trusted them to look after her daughter. Living with them was pleasant for the most part. They treated Samara like family, and took good care of her, just as her mother had promised.

The last family was the worst. They did not treat their foster children the way the Carlton's had. In fact, there was very little interaction with the family. The big house had six bedrooms, a family room, and a finished basement. Antique furniture graced the rooms on the main floor, but the children were not permitted to enter those rooms. Samara spent most of her time on the third floor, confined to her bedroom.

At meal times, the foster children ate in the kitchen by themselves, after the family. Breakfast was always the same—store brand Corn Flakes scooped out and placed in plastic bowls by the foster mother. It never changed. Dinner wasn't much better. They would have tuna casserole or something similar, after the family had finished their steak and potatoes. Even so, the children were never mistreated, and Samara was grateful for that.

Samara and the other foster children were locked in their bedrooms at night. That was so they wouldn't go roaming about the house when everyone was sleeping. The only time Samara was not locked in her room was when Aunt Sarah visited.

Every other weekend she shared her room with a woman named Aunt Sarah. She was not her real aunt. Aunt Sarah was a spinster, and a very unhappy one at that. Samara never saw the woman smile. At bedtime, Samara was instructed to lie on her side facing the wall. She was not to move for any reason—not even to go to the bathroom. She had to remain completely still the entire night.

Aunt Sarah did not like having the windows open, and always made a point of closing the blinds and curtains. The room would be so black that Samara was not able to see her hand in front of her. Samara hated those weekends, and would beg God to let Sunday come quickly.

Samara wanted desperately to be with her mother. She longed to be happy like her friends at school, and spent countless hours daydreaming about what it must be like to live with her very own mother and father.

She finally ran away, in search of her mother.

For if the trumpet give an uncertain sound, who shall prepare himself for the battle?
—1 Corinthians 14:8 (KJV)

Chapter Xv

"My lord, we've come to give our report on Thumar."

"Let's hear it then. What has my little friend been up to these days?" Mastema interrogated the soldiers.

"We trailed him to the grandmother's house," another warrior offered. "He waited a long time before going in. There was no reason for the delayed entry because the humans were gone. We think Thumar may suspect something."

"Excellent." It was not a compliment.

Mastema drew his sword, inspecting the jeweled handle. He did not intend to use it at that moment, but it was good to keep the subordinates guessing. There was to be no question as to who was in charge.

"Did you observe any other suspicious activity?" He demanded.

"Yes, my lord. Thumar was not alone in the house."

"Make up your mind! You just reported that the house was empty. Which is it?"

The soldiers shuddered noticeably, chancing a sideways glance at each other. They were beginning to feel like pawns in a very elaborate game. It was not in their best interest to be caught in the middle of whatever this was.

"It appears that Thumar has enlisted the aid of a fellow warrior," the division captain spoke up.

"Perhaps our loyal soldier has decided to head up some sort of conspiracy?" Mastema taunted his audience. "Are you sure there was only one other?"

"There was only one other soldier with Thumar. It was Putnah," The captain continued, answering their commander.

"Yes, of course … the puny one that has been refused entry amongst our upper echelon. Apparently, he has resorted to acquiring access some other way. I want a unit assigned to Putnah immediately!"

"It's as good as done, my lord."

"We won't take any chances on his siphoning information from inside sources. Whatever he knows, he is sure to blab to Thumar. He will do anything to become second in command of their pathetic little uprising. Any chance Putnah knows they're being trailed?"

"Not likely. He was too careless in approaching the house."

"Stupid fools," Mastema hissed. "And you're sure they never spotted you?"

"We were careful not to blow our cover, my lord. We stayed behind at a safe distance until they both left the human's house."

"And the guardian?" Mastema turn his sword over very slowly, causing the jewels to give off an eerie glow.

"He was nearby. But as you said, he did not interfere."

"Consider yourselves lucky." Mastema mocked the small contingent: "Had Lariel *interfered* none of you would have survived to deliver your report."

Mastema placed his sword on the table and examined the soldiers standing before him. The information they had given was not news. He had gotten wind of a plot to overthrow his position. The squadron charged with watching Thumar was also under Mastema's scrutiny. He trusted no one. Hadn't he eliminated other hopefuls to obtain his position?

"If Thumar has enlisted the aid of underlings, and I suspect that he has," Mastema continued, "then he is sure to have set up a command post. How unfortunate for him. He could have been very useful. Who's trailing him now?"

"My lord," The higher-ranking officer spoke, "I have dispatched my best soldiers. They will report back to me immediately with any new developments."

"Make sure they do." Mastema recovered the sword and pointed it at the captain. "Or your head will be delivered to me on a platter."

The captain hastily evacuated the interrogation room with his soldiers in tow.

*I keep asking that the God of our Lord Jesus Christ, the glorious
Father, may give you the Spirit of wisdom and revelation, so that
you may know him better. I pray also that the eyes of your heart
may be enlightened in order that you may know the hope to which
he has called you, the riches of his glorious inheritance in the
saints, and his incomparably great power for us who believe.*
—*Ephesians 1:17-19a (NIV)*

Chapter XVI

"THIS IS *NOT* A date." Samara insisted as she eyed her friend Lourdes through the full-length mirror that was perched above the Victorian dresser in her bedroom.

She twirled a small section of her hair around the sizzling curling iron. It had been a while since she had put this much effort into styling her hair, and she was growing impatient. The last thing she needed right now was to burn her ear lobe. She took a deep breath and curled another section.

Noah had called earlier in the week to say that he had found several books on the subject of spiritual warfare that he thought might be helpful, and had asked if it would be okay to discuss the matter over coffee. Samara had been surprised to hear from him so soon after her visit to the church. She had figured that her name was most likely at the bottom of his 'crazy people to check on' list. Nevertheless, she promptly accepted the invitation before his secretary discovered the obvious mix-up.

Lourdes had come over to provide moral support, and to set the record straight. Of course, this was her official duty as the best friend. She had determined that Samara would need major help preparing for the rendezvous. It had been more than twenty years since Samara had kept company with someone other than Tony, and Lu was not about to miss the big event.

Samara gave up on the curling iron and set it down on its stand. Her curls looked lopsided and crazy, as if her hair had a will of its own. At this point, it was what it was—a hot mess. She ransacked her jewelry chest in search of the perfect ensemble to match the empire-waist, maxi dress presently draped across Lu's lap. The floral, spaghetti-strapped outfit had cost Samara a small fortune several years back, but she had never worn it. It had been another casualty of her lackluster social life. The matching silk jacket still had the price tags dangling from its sleeves.

"Sounds like a date to me, mommy." Lu rebutted, as she snipped the tags off the jacket. "Last time I checked, pastors generally provide counseling at the church, not some cozy café."

"I'd hardly call the Starbucks in the Barnes and Noble downtown, *cozy*." Samara chuckled. "This is the middle of the week. And, it's lunchtime. The whole world will be there, eating lunch and clicking away on their laptops. Besides, I'm guessing he chose a public place because he'd rather I not bring those demons back onto the church premises."

"It still sounds suspicious." Lu said as she draped the tag-free outfit across the back of the chair. "When you get there, don't be surprised if he's sitting in the booth, in the back, in the corner…"

"Not if I get there first." Samara interjected.

"I love you Sam, but you know that that's not gonna happen. When are you ever the first to arrive anywhere? I'm just saying… it smells like a date to me."

"Well it's not, so you can stop sniffing. Besides, who says that Noah is even available? It's possible that he's already seeing somebody."

"Noah?" Lu raised her newly tweezed eyebrows. "Since when did we get to be on a first name basis with the good reverend?"

"Since he insisted that I not call him Reverend." Samara reached for the COCO Mademoiselle—her favorite Chanel perfume. "Besides, he's not *my* pastor."

"Yeah, but he *is* providing some kind of spiritual guidance, isn't he? Just seems like the church office is the best place for that kind of thing; provided, of course, that this isn't a date."

Samara turned from the mirror to face her best friend head-on. She tightened the belt to her bathrobe, and shoved her hands deep into the fuzzy pockets. This matter would be settled for the last time. As far as she was concerned, she was simply meeting Noah to discuss her most recent dreams, and to purchase a few books. There might be a latte or two involved, but nothing more. Although, she had to admit that it *was* odd that he had asked to meet at Starbucks. And, she *was* a bit anxious, now that she thought about it.

"I will confess that I was a little surprised when *Noah* asked that we meet away from the church…" Samara paused, as though realizing something for the first time. "I had assumed that whenever I saw him again that it would be in his office."

"That's exactly what I'm saying." Lu reiterated. "I'm thinking that this might be a little more than a counseling session. You're single, he's single…"

"Okay, okay. I hear you." Samara acquiesced. "Getting together in a social setting could be construed as something more casual than meeting in the pastor's office. I guess I hadn't really thought about it like that."

"You're so formal." Lu smiled at her friend. "But I get it. You're still protecting yourself. If anybody understands, I do. I have walked through this ugly mess with you. But it's been three years since the divorce. Tony has moved on. It's time for you to do the same. Why don't you give yourself permission to believe that something good could actually happen to you?"

"I know. Nana has been saying the same thing." Samara hesitated. "But what could a well-respected, man-of-the-cloth possibly see in me; especially after I've regurgitated my issues all over his office?"

"Are you kidding?" Lourdes encouraged her friend. "You're more than a divorced mom who also happens to be experiencing close encounters of the strangest kind."

"Don't forget the unemployed, and living with her elderly grandmother, part."

"Sam, this is the only life you get down here. Please take some time to smell the roses while you can. You have suffered through some pretty painful stuff. It's time to embrace the joyful moments. Stop punishing yourself. That is not God's will for you, or me. Believe it or not, He really does want us to enjoy our lives."

"Maybe so, but I didn't get that memo."

"Don't start…"

"I'm sorry." Samara offered an apologetic smile. "You're right. Old habits die hard. It's just that I've been in this holding pattern for so long that it has become my new normal. I don't like it, but it's familiar. I know *this* pain. When an unexpected wind of happiness blows my way, I'm looking over my shoulder for the disappointment that inevitably follows. I figure it's just a matter of time. Why get up, only to be knocked down again?"

"Oh, Sam." Lourdes heart ached for her friend. "I'm so sorry that you've had to endure such loss. But it's never God's intention to use these things to destroy us. He allows them to happen; but, at the same time, He is doing something wonderful in us. I mean, think about it. Did you ever think that you'd come through all of this with your sanity still intact?"

"It's questionable as to whether or not my sanity is intact." Samara chuckled. "But, I must admit that I've discovered strength I didn't know I had. When TJ died, it felt like a part of me had died with him. When Tony decided that he didn't want to be married, I died a little bit more. I didn't think that I could make it without my husband by my side."

"But you have, my dear sister."

Lourdes got up from the chair, walked over to where Samara stood, and hugged her neck. It was a moment of friend bonding with friend, and of friendship evolving into sisterhood.

"Starting over is seldom easy." Lourdes grabbed her hands. "The wind of change often brings with it a fear of the unknown. But thank God for the hope of every new beginning."

* * *

Midday traffic on the West River Drive seemed unusually heavy. Driving was proving to be the least effective mode of transportation. Samara was stuck in the bumper-to-bumper melee, staring mindlessly at the rowers practicing for the Schuylkill Regatta. She watched as their canoes glided gracefully down the river; their oars moving in synchronized rhythm.

Lunchtime joggers sprinted along Boat House Row, dodging the toddlers that were frolicking in the grass under the watchful eye of their mothers. Life was in motion for everyone except the impatient commuters stuck in their cars. Samara honked her horn at the driver in the lane next to her. His car was drifting dangerously close to hers. The distracted gentleman had one eye on the road and the other on his mobile phone.

"Stop texting and drive." Samara mumbled.

She could see the Cira Center looming in the distance. The multi-angular, silver glass skyscraper was built on a platform over the rail tracks across from 30th Street Station, and could be seen from every direction. It also served as Samara's two-mile benchmark. She would need to get in the far right lane very shortly. Her exit was coming up.

She maneuvered her way across two lanes and exited at the southbound ramp heading toward Broad St. The bookstore was off Walnut, so she didn't have much further to go. As luck would have it, someone was pulling out of a parking space just as Samara was nearing her destination. She edged the nose of her Mustang into the space while the other car was still partially in it. That's how it's done in the city. If you snooze, you lose.

The clock at the historic City Hall building chimed one time. Samara was officially late. She finished parking, grabbed her purse, and exited the car in search of the nearest parking meter kiosk. Fortunately, it was only two car lengths away. After swiping her debit card and punching in her pin number, she took the receipt and placed it in a prominent place on the front dashboard inside her car.

I should have suggested that we stick with meeting at the church. This is way too much effort for a latte. I could have ordered the books on line.

Samara quickened her pace as she rounded the corner at the intersection of Broad and Walnut. She was glad that she had worn flat sandals. The concrete pavements were no joke. Stepping inside the bookstore, she stood off to the side so that she could get her bearings. It was her first time visiting this particular location.

Someone was standing at the top of the second level landing, waving in her direction. It took a few moments for her to realize that it was Noah. He looked different from what she had remembered. Samara waved back and headed for the stairs.

It suddenly dawned on her that she hadn't paid much attention to his appearance during her visit to the church. Frankly, she had not cared what Noah looked like, or how old he was, or if he was single. She just needed help.

But the Noah waiting for her at the top of the stairs was disturbingly appealing. He looked different somehow.

Why am I so nervous all of a sudden? Lift up your dress so you don't trip up the steps. Remain calm.

"You've made it here alive, I see." Noah's smile was instantly engaging.

"Barely." Samara returned the greeting as she cleared the last step. "I can't believe the hordes of people milling around out there. You'd think that nobody's working today."

That's right. Keep it professional.

"Everyone's most likely enjoying the last of our Indian summer." Noah said. "Our table is over here. I lucked out on a prime spot away from the cluster."

Samara followed him to their appointed meeting place. It wasn't exactly in the corner, in the back. It wasn't even a booth. Yet, it allowed for a decent amount of privacy, considering the three-level store was packed to the brim with customers.

Noah pulled the chair out and helped her into her seat.

"Can I get you something?" He offered before sitting down. "My secretary offered up the church's American Express card, so I can splurge just a little bit."

"In that case," Samara answered without hesitation, "I'll have a Grande Caramel Macchiato, and a slice of the iced lemon pound cake."

"Now there's a woman who knows what she wants." Noah flashed the charismatic smile and headed for the Starbucks counter. "I'll be right back."

This guy is a perfect gentleman. And what a smile. It lights up his entire face.

Samara took the opportunity to give her lunch companion a quick once-over. If she had to guess, she would say that Noah was about five-feet-eleven in height, maybe six-feet at the most. Either way, he looked to be in good shape. The business-casual attire suited him perfectly. His fitted, blue-striped shirt was open at the collar, and was an ideal choice for the grayish blue Dockers. It looked as if the shirt and pants were new, or just out of the cleaners. There was not a wrinkle in sight. The polished black shoes looked to be standard oxford tie-ups. The only jewelry he sported was a beautiful platinum watch.

Something about this guy...

Samara looked down at her cell phone and pretended to be reading as Noah headed back to the table.

"Two caramel macchiato and one slice of lemon pound cake." He placed the food on the table.

"Thank you." Samara took a quick sip of the hot drink. "This is delicious."

"So," Noah pulled out the chair across from her and sat down, "let's get down to business. How are things? Have you had any more special dreams?"

"As a matter of fact, I have." Samara set the hot drink on the table. "This time it was about my father. However, I am beginning to notice a common thread. My nemesis is always the same. He disguises himself each time, but I still recognize him."

"Are you sure it's the same entity?" Noah seemed genuinely intrigued.

"I'm very sure. He knows me, and I know him. It is as if the masquerade is over. Game on—so to speak."

"So, we're saying that this entity has personally targeted you, and has chosen to show up in your dream-state for the purpose of delivering these cryptic messages."

"Wow. When you put it like that, it sounds a lot more credible."

"These books have really shed some light on the subject of spiritual warfare. When I cross referenced the information with what the bible says, I was blown away."

Samara took a bite of the lemon cake, allowing a few moments of silence to pass between them. She considered the significance of what Noah was saying. His orientation toward her situation had noticeably changed since their last meeting. He'd obviously had some sort of epiphany.

"You're a pastor." She broke the silence. "Isn't this sort of thing a little more commonplace for you?"

"I'll be the first to admit that I've never done more than a topical study on the subject. I believe that angels and demons exist and that they are involved with the affairs of our world; but I've never dug much deeper than that."

Samara traced the pattern on her napkin as she considered her next move. She had hoped that Noah would be the one to point her in the right direction. Now it seemed that he had as much learning to do on this subject as she had. The blind was leading the blind.

"Before we go any further," Noah interrupted her wandering thoughts, "I think that you should take these books home and read them along with your bible. I would rather not suggest anything more specific than that right now. Something is definitely happening, and I don't want to muddy the waters with faulty speculation. I don't mean to get all religious or anything, but it seems to me that God has made it His business to get your attention."

"How can you be so sure that it's God, when all I've seen are demons?"

"That's just it." Noah looked her straight on. "If God weren't up to something, you wouldn't be having these encounters with this entity. That's what the fight is about. Think about it. The presence of that demon only serves to give credibility to the presence of God in some other way."

"Some other way? " Samara was puzzled. "Like what?"

"Like angels." Noah hesitated for effect. "The bible gives specific reference to guardian angels being assigned to those of us who are to be heirs of salvation."

Samara blinked back at Noah in rapid succession. This was more information than she could handle in one sitting. She was still coming to grips with the idea of dark spirits lurking in her dreams. She had never considered the possibility of good angels hanging around to boot. And what was all this talk about being an heir? She had lost everything. But it made sense somehow. In fact, it made so much sense that she wondered why she had not thought of it on her own.

"Then why haven't I seen these good angels in my dreams?" She still needed further confirmation.

"Do you know for certain that you haven't?" Noah persisted.

Samara sat straight up in her chair. An image flashed through her mind at the speed of light. She had forgotten all about it until that very moment. The beautiful being had appeared in her dream the other night.

"I can't believe it." She shook her head as if dislodging the image. "I did see something, and it spoke to me. It was so comforting."

"And there you have it."

"All I have are more questions."

"No—what you have is a clearer picture. You've seen more than your realize Samara. You have been granted insight into something that eludes most of us. It's up to you to seek out the answers."

"Now you're sounding like my grandmother."

"Then I'm in good company. I would suggest that you commit this to serious prayer. You might also consider attending our weekly bible study on Wednesday evenings. We do an in depth, verse-by-verse examination of the scriptures. Maybe we'll start a new series on the subject of angels. I think we'd all benefit from it."

"It can't hurt. I'm feeling a little overwhelmed right now."

"Don't panic. I believe that we are on the right track. The answer will come in time."

"Time is all I've got right now so I guess I'd better spend it well."

"Sounds good." Noah prepared to leave. "I must be getting along. The trustee board meets this afternoon. They don't like to be kept waiting. We'll see you next Wednesday night at seven?"

"I think so."

"Great. Are you parked close by? I'll walk you to your car."

"Thanks, but I want to look around the store and maybe check out other books on the subject."

"Good idea." He rose from the chair. "Well, I've truly enjoyed this."

"Me too." Samara offered her hand. "See you Wednesday."

She watched him as he made his way to the stairway. His stride was purposeful and confident.

Something about him...

Though I walk in the midst of trouble, you will preserve my life, you stretch out your hand against the anger of my foes, with your right hand you save me.
—*Psalms 138:7 (NIV)*

Chapter XVII

The van pulled up to the church exactly fifteen minutes before service started. It was the same every Sunday, just like clockwork. They made their way inside, nodding and saying their good mornings, with Matt bringing up the rear. It was his responsibility to see to it that everyone was present and accounted for. New Life's policy required the men to sit together in the same section of the church. Their row of seats was generally available, thanks to the capable ushers.

Matt was okay with going to church to fulfill an obligation. The whole religion thing, however, never had appealed to him. Other folks needed to believe in some greater power, but he wanted something more substantial than an invisible, ethereal being who promised to let you go to heaven if you were a good girl or boy. His rap sheet gave testament to the life he had lived. He wasn't feeling the "Jesus" story either, and he was sure the feeling was mutual. This God would not be interested in someone like him.

Matt admired Pastor Bromley though. Something about the man rang true. He seemed straight up, like a regular kind of guy. His sermons were decent; sometimes a little long, but not bad. Matt appreciated how easy it was to approach the reverend. Their conversations were usually short, but meaningful. He didn't waste Matt's time with pretentious, phony conversation.

The members were okay people too. They were a little touchy–feely for his taste, but good folks nonetheless. It was the most hug-loving group of people he had ever met. Someone was forever shaking his hands and calling him Brother Matthew. After two years, he simply learned to deal with it. His smile and handshake become more genuine in the process, without his even realizing it.

He secretly envied the families filing into the church every Sunday. Everyone looked nice and cared for. The drone of friendly chatter that resounded throughout the sanctuary was very comforting in an inexplicable way. It was as if the cares and troubles of the world were on hold for those two hours per week.

Matt enjoyed observing normal people, especially younger parents trying desperately to control their fidgeting children. Or the grandmother that inevitably came to everybody's rescue. He would watch the same misbehaving kids crawl up on their parents' laps and be enveloped in pure love. It represented something that seemed forever out of Matt's reach. They were family, and they were together.

Church used to give Matt the creeps. He didn't attend Sunday school when he was growing up. No one ever took him. The only times he went were when somebody was getting married or had died. Prior to attending Asbury, the last time he had stepped foot inside was for his best friend, Steve's funeral. They had been inseparable since childhood. He was only nineteen when he died in Matt's arms from a drug overdose.

Not long afterward, Matt had begun having dreams about his dead friend. He had awakened many nights with the burning image of his buddy lying in the casket. The scene was always the same—Matt would be sitting in the same pew, looking down at his friend. Steve's eyes would spring open and he would begin speaking. He remembered the urgency in his friend's eyes, but he could not remember what he had said. The dreams eventually stopped.

"Good morning, gentlemen. Glad to see you all this morning."

Noah had been making his way around the sanctuary, greeting the parishioners before the start of service.

"Morning, Pastor," the men responded in varying tempos.

"Everybody staying out of trouble?" Noah asked.

"It's all good." Matt answered for the group.

"You're looking pretty sharp there, brother Dante."

"Don't I though, Reverend?" Dante flashed his signature grin. "I'm trying to represent for the group. These guys don't know the difference between Armani and Versace. I mean, really."

"Somebody's gotta do it." Noah played along. "Might as well be you. Keep up the good work."

It was a good thing for Dante that the men were in church, in the presence of the good reverend. Otherwise, he would have heard a few choice words that would have surely caused the elderly saints sitting nearby to move to another section.

"Mind if I speak with you a second?" Noah motioned to Matt.

"Sure thing, Rev."

He followed the pastor to the rear of the sanctuary.

"Listen," Noah started, "we really need some help in the parking lot today. I know this is not your scheduled Sunday, but we are a little short. Would you mind?"

"If you need me, I'm available."

"Well, we certainly need you today." Noah responded. "Brother Dave called the office this morning and told the secretary that he wouldn't be able to make it to service today. The kids all have the flu. You know how that goes."

"I can only imagine." Matt offered. "I'll head on over to the security booth."

"Thanks buddy." Noah patted his shoulder. "Appreciate it. Grab some coffee and donuts from the fellowship hall when you come back in."

"Sure thing."

Actually, Matt didn't know what it was like to be a part of a normal family. His mother and father had never married. They had been together for years as a family when his father decided that he no longer wanted to "live in sin." He had become one of those "new-borns," and it was against their religion to shack up. His pastor had encouraged him to either marry his mother or move out of the house. He moved out.

Matt had neither seen nor heard from his father since, except for the child support checks that came every month. He found out much later that his father had married another woman and had more children.

But Jesus immediately said to them; "Take courage! It is I. Do not be afraid."
—Matthew 14:27 (NIV)

Chapter XVIII

Samara helped her grandmother into the car and loaded her walker in the trunk. They were going to Asbury together on this particular Sunday. A deacon had called the house earlier in the week to schedule a convenient time to come and give communion, but Anna had advised the nice man that she was going to the church. She had missed too many services and nothing was going to get in her way—not even sickness.

"You look very nice today, dear." Anna adjusted her seatbelt. "It's good to see you looking like my granddaughter again."

"I fixed myself up a little. You always said that if you look good, you feel good. There seems to be some truth to that. I must admit that today seems a little better than yesterday."

"This wouldn't have anything to do with seeing the pastor again, now would it?"

"Don't start, Nana. It was a counseling session. That's all."

"Well, he is a great listener. He's not hard on the eyes either."

"Nana!"

"Honey, your grandmother might be old, but she ain't blind. Listen, you have been by yourself long enough. It's time to come out from under that rock."

"I like my secluded place. It's safe and familiar, just the way I like it."

"You've punished yourself long enough honey." Anna held her granddaughter's stare. "It'd do you some good to start keeping company again."

"Self-imposed isolation isn't necessarily punishment. I'm just more comfortable dealing with known issues right now. New relationships require a level of emotional stability, of which I am devoid. Besides, after twenty-five years of marriage, my tolerance level is a little low. Anyway, he's too busy with the church to have time for something as trivial as dating."

"He's a man first, honey." Anna patted her granddaughter's arm.

"A man of the cloth, you mean. I've got too much drama going on for that."

"Don't be so quick to count yourself out."

"Who's counting?" Samara asked. "And who says I'm even interested?"

She had to admit that her visits with Pastor Bromley had proven more helpful than she had hoped. At least he hadn't gone all-religious and start flashing a cross. She had been sure he was going to reach for some hidden buzzer when she had first told him about the angels and demons. He probably had to decide whether to have his security escort her crazy self off the church premises.

"Well at least you've given him a chance to help." Her grandmother gently prodded.

Samara turned into the church parking lot and headed toward the main entrance.

"Oh look," Anna pointed to the attendant approaching their car, "there's that nice young man."

"Who is he?" Samara peeped over her sunglasses.

"His name is Matthew. He sits in the same section I do, and always makes it a point to speak. Very gracious."

"Interesting." Samara unlocked the door just as Matt arrived at the passenger side.

"Morning ladies." He greeted them with a full smile as he opened the car door. "Good to see you Mrs. M."

"Good morning Matthew," Anna returned the favor. "It's a blessing to be here on such a beautiful day. This is my granddaughter, Samara. She's visiting with us today."

"Welcome to Asbury." Matt nodded at Samara. "Do you have your walker today, Mrs. M.?"

"I sure do. It's in the trunk."

Samara pressed the release button and got out of the car. She walked to the passenger side and reached for her grandmother.

"I got her." Matt closed the trunk and positioned the walker.

Samara watched him handle her grandmother with effortless precision. Other cars were lining up behind theirs, but Matt attended to Anna as if no one else were there. He walked alongside her, smiling and nodding as they made their way inside.

Samara got back in the car and pulled off in search of a parking space. They were a little early, so there were still a few good spaces left. She was reaching for her things when she spotted Matthew coming toward her. Something in his expression alarmed her. He was no longer smiling.

"It's your grandmother." His voice was calm and measured. "She's asking for you."

"Is something wrong?" Samara already knew.

"I'm not sure." Matt turned and headed back inside the church.

"What happened?"

"We were making our way into the sanctuary when she suddenly asks me to help her to the visitor's lounge. When I asked her if she was okay, she said that she didn't want to draw any attention, but asked that I please go and get you."

Matt and Samara hurried into the visitor's lounge, where they found Anna collapsed and unconscious on the floor.

* * *

The emergency room smelled of fresh paint and industrial strength disinfectant.

Samara sat in the waiting area, staring mindlessly at three mounted flat screen televisions. Three different reporters rendered their perspectives on the same bad news.

A preoccupied dad sat off to the side, typing away on his laptop. His teenage daughter was in the back with what was most likely the flu. The sound of his fingers tapping on the keyboard was driving Samara batty. She wished she could use the TV remote to mute the impatient father.

Matt had driven Samara to the hospital in her car and had insisted on staying until he was sure that she was not alone. He had even called and left an update for Pastor Bromley. They drank coffee and made small talk while they waited.

"I feel awful that you're missing church." Samara apologized again.

It's not a problem." Matt smiled reassuringly. "I wouldn't have it any other way. Your grandmother is a very sweet lady."

"She wanted to come out so badly. I thought she was strong enough, but I guess she's gotten really good at masking the pain."

"Haven't we all."

It wasn't *what* he said that caused Samara to see Matt for the first time, but it was *how* he said it. Something in the tone of his voice suggested that he was no stranger to suffering. Yet he was there, selflessly attending to someone else's need. She could see why her grandmother thought so highly of him. He displayed a rare and genuine kindness. Samara made a mental note to leave a thank you card for him at the church.

"At least let me offer my car so you can get back." She held out the keys.

"You'd trust me with your baby? That's a nice little car you've got there."

"Not everybody can drive a stick shift." Samara smiled for the first time since arriving at the hospital. "You handled her like a pro."

"Let's just say I've driven my share of cars," Matt confessed. "But really, I can have one of the guys pick me up in the van."

"Stop fighting it!" Samara teased him. "Take the car. My parents will drive me home."

Brian and Elinor Louis, Samara's mother and stepfather, had gotten there only a few short minutes after they had.

"What about your car?" Matt was still hesitant.

"My dad will pick it up later."

"Well," he said, caving, "if you're sure."

Matt took the keys and recorded her number in his phone. He promised to call her as soon as her car was back at the church, safe and sound.

"I know where to find you." Samara said.

Her parents returned from the nurses' station. They had asked to speak with the doctor, but he was still working on getting Samara's grandmother stabilized. No one was allowed to go to her room until then. The triage nurse had promised to keep them as informed as possible.

"Who was that guy with you?" Elinor dug right in.

"A member of Nana's church." Samara didn't bother resisting. "He drove me here."

"He seems nice." Brian Louis offered a rare opinion.

"Nana thinks so. He was helping her inside right before she collapsed."

"He asked for your number?" Elinor persisted.

"Leave it alone, babe," her husband countered.

Samara closed her eyes and offered up a small prayer. It's what her nana would do. She managed a few brief, unintelligent phrases. It had been a while since she had prayed in earnest for someone other than herself or the kids.

Her pocketbook buzzed on her lap. The cell phone had been on vibrate since early that morning. She reached inside the bag and checked the number. It didn't belong to anyone on her contact list. The caller was "Unknown." It could be Matt. She had not programmed his number yet. But he could not possibly have gotten to the church that quickly. He better not had.

"Hello?" This would have to be quick.

She heard someone breathing, but the person was not saying anything. He or she had one more chance.

"Hello?" She tried again.

"Samara?"

It was her turn to be speechless. This was not happening.

"Sam, is that you?" He wasn't really asking.

"Yes?" Her brain was working, but her mouth refused to cooperate.

"I'm sorry," Tony continued, "Did I catch you at a bad time?"

Samara held the phone at arm's length, staring at it as if it were a foreign object. There was no way she could handle this right now. Her heart was beating as if she had run a marathon.

For three years, she had practiced an award-worthy monologue of what she would say if she ever got the chance. Here it was, at the worst possible time ever. If this was somebody's idea of a joke, she was not laughing.

A look of abject confusion settled across her face. The dazed expression moved from her mother, to her stepdad, and back to her phone. The moment of reckoning was not supposed to happen like this.

"What is it, honey?" her mother asked.

"I'm not sure." Samara blinked uncontrollably. "It's Tony."

"Your husband?"

"*Ex*-husband. And yes, that Tony."

"Well dear, see what he wants. It must be important."

Samara placed the phone up to her ear. He was still on the line. She could hear his breathing.

"Tony?"

"It sounds like you have a lot going on." He said. "I can call back when it's more convenient."

"It's okay." Samara was having difficulty pronouncing more than three syllables at a time.

"I'll be quick. My mom gave me your number. I hope that was okay."

"No. I mean, it's not a problem." Her tongue was finally loosening. "Yes, it's okay."

Elinor eyed her daughter from across the room with a look that said, *Get it together.*

"I wouldn't blame you for hanging up on me," Tony pleaded, "but at least hear me out first."

"I'm listening." Samara rolled her eyes upward.

"It's hard to believe it's been three years, but better late than never, I guess." He paused. "I was thinking that it's time to reconnect with the kids. It seemed like a good idea to check with you first, so, that's why I'm calling."

"Okay …"

"So … would you be terribly opposed to meeting somewhere so that we can talk about this? I'd rather not discuss it over the phone."

"Can you hold one second?"

He hesitated. "Sure."

Samara pushed the mute button, shoved the phone in her pocketbook, and zipped it up—just to be sure. Her mother sat at attention, waiting for the verdict.

"Mom, can you believe he has the nerve to call my phone and ask about getting together? All of a sudden, he wants to talk about the kids—three years later? Since when did he start caring about them?"

Elinor remained silent. Brian watched.

"And what exactly am I supposed to do?" Samara rushed on. "He calls out of the clear blue, and I'm supposed to say okay, just like that? Really?"

"What's at stake?" Elinor stopped the gushing.

"I'm not confused on the issue. If I tell him no, then the kids pay. If I tell him yes, then I get to relive the past three years."

"Do you still love him, Samara?" Elinor stared her down.

"Why does everybody keep asking me that? I am so done with him."

"Are you?"

"Look, I don't want anything to do with Tony. Moreover, I resent the fact that he thinks he can drop in out of nowhere and disrupt everybody's lives. We're supposed to just go ahead and accommodate him because he's ready to be a father again? He gets to pick and choose?"

Her stepdad interrupted the heated conversation, which surprised Samara and her mother. He normally stayed out of their disagreements.

"Like it or not, they're his kids too," he opined. "You can't change that. I am telling you that those kids need their father. Therefore, you can either handle this like an adult or continue to hold your children hostage. Your call."

"Thanks honey," Elinor smiled at her husband. "She wouldn't have heard me if I'd said it."

Samara unzipped her pocketbook, retrieved the cell phone, and released the mute button.

"Sorry about that." She offered the half-hearted apology.

"That's okay." Tony exhaled. "I'm just glad you didn't hang up. So what's it gonna be?"

"What did you have in mind?"

Let us not become weary in doing good, for in the proper time we will reap a harvest if we do not give up.
—Galatians 6:19 (NIV)

Chapter XIX

Samara stepped into the darkness of her grandmother's house, locking the door behind her. She disengaged the alarm and dropped her keys and handbag on the Planters of Dorking table. Maximus greeted her with short, indignant yelps. His fluffy tail thumped against the hardwood floor. They had been gone all day.

"Hi, Max." She kicked off her shoes. "Were you holding down the fort?"

Pale blue moonlight streamed through the windows, illuminating a path that led toward the kitchen. That would have to do for now. Groping for a lamp required energy she did not have. Samara stood motionless in the middle of the room, too exhausted to think. The long, grueling day had taken its toll. She closed her eyes and released the tension she had been holding since that morning.

Her stepfather had brought her home so that she could get some rest. They would leave her car at the church overnight. Noah had been kind enough to call for an update on her grandmother and to let her know that the security staff would look after her car. He promised to stop by the hospital after he closed up the church. Members of the clergy were not restricted to regular visiting hours.

Samara headed for the kitchen in search of dinner for herself and the dog. Poor Max had not eaten all day. He was right on her heels. She grabbed the bag of his favorite food from the pantry and mixed it just the way he liked it. For an extra treat, she threw in a piece of leftover meat loaf.

"Here you go." She set his bowl on the floor: "A special meal for a special friend."

Max wasted no time digging in. His dog tags clinked against the dish as he devoured his meal. She filled his other bowl with cold tap water and grabbed a few ice cubes from the freezer. Max did not like warm water.

Samara fixed herself a cup of tea and made a sandwich with the rest of the meat loaf. It wasn't exactly what she'd had in mind, but her grandmother's leftovers tasted even better the second time around. She ate her meal at the table just as she had that morning. Everything was as it had been, except that her nana had not returned with her.

She watched Max nudge his treat to the side of the bowl with his nose. He was saving it for last. Being a dog must be so easy, she thought. You eat, poop, sleep, and play. How hard can that be?

When they had both finished eating, Samara let Max out the back door and cleaned up the kitchen. He returned to the porch just as she was putting the last of the dishes away.

"Let's secure the house, Max."

She wanted to make sure all the doors and windows were locked before turning in. It had never bothered her before, but she was feeling a bit vulnerable in the big house alone. They would begin at the bottom and work their way up.

As they reached the basement landing, Max suddenly froze. His hair stood on his back as he positioned himself in front of Samara. He started growling and barking.

"Settle down, Max. We're the only ones here."

Samara flipped the switch on the wall. It was her first time down there since moving in. A lone, sixty-watt bulb dangled from the ceiling, providing the only light. She could see the entire basement from where she stood. The room spanned the length of the house and was in varying stages of renovation. Her grandfather had been working on fixing it up before he took sick.

She tried to move past the German shepherd, but he blocked her path.

"Move out of the way, Max!" She stepped over him. "And hush up. You'll wake the neighbors."

He continued barking in the direction of the door that led to the outside. It was at the back of the room near the laundry area. The dim bulb did not give off enough light to penetrate the shadows. Samara shushed the dog again as she moved away from the steps to check the locks.

The steel door was dead-bolted on both sides. No one could get in or out unless they had the key, which hung on the hook next to the washer and dryer. Samara turned the knob to make sure that it was locked. It wasn't.

Max came up behind her, still barking and growling. Samara could see the membrane in the back of his eyes illuminating through the semidarkness. She snatched the key from the hook and quickly locked the door. There was no way of knowing how long it had been unlocked. She placed the key in her pocket and retreated up the steps.

Samara shut the door to the basement and returned to the kitchen. She was suddenly very afraid. They had not checked the rest of the house. Her heart beat wildly in her chest. The big house pulsed with kinetic energy. She had an eerie feeling that she was not alone. It was all too familiar, except this time she was not dreaming.

* * *

Thumar and Putnah leered at each other in the dark corners of the basement. Their plan was working. The door had been unlocked all along, but the stupid human couldn't think past her own fears. The animal was smarter than the female.

"By the time we're finished with the human, she'll be afraid of her own shadow." Thumar bragged. "The only truth she'll believe is that the "bogeyman" is after her."

"And then what, my lord?" Putnah asked.

Thumar reveled in his newly elevated authority. The self-appointed leader was quite pleased with his progress. There was still much to be accomplished, but he was not ready to reveal the whole plan to the inferiors. Their loyalty must first be proven. Putnah would have his chance tonight. The little demon was eager to move up within the ranks.

"You will know more when I tell you!" Thumar roared.

"I did not mean to anger you."

"Don't let it happen again, or you will face the wrath of ..."

The new commander stopped mid-sentence. He sensed, rather than saw, a movement in the darkness. The hairs on his back tingled down his leathery spine.

"What is it?" Putnah withdrew further into the shadows.

"Shut up you fool!" Thumar whispered.

Whether it was Lariel or some of Mastema's henchmen, he was not sure. They had yet to reveal themselves. He slowly drew his sword from its sheath. It was a mistake.

Two of the fiercest warring angels he had ever seen appeared before them. Gabriel had dispatched them from his command post.

"You are to leave this place immediately." It was all they intended to say.

"Where is Lariel?" Thumar demanded.

The angels gave no response. Their swords remained poised.

"Who sent you?" Putnah spluttered.

With that, the angels joined their swords at the tips. Thumar pushed Putnah in front of him.

"Stop whimpering and fight you coward! It is your duty to protect your commander!"

Putnah reached for his sword. This would secure his entrance into the upper ranks. He never saw the strike coming. The shorter of the two angels pierced him through the side. The demon fell backwards, his hand still groping for his weapon.

He staggered to his feet stunned and confused. The wound was bleeding profusely, but he would prove his combat readiness to Thumar.

"We tell you once more." The angels warned. "Leave this place at once!"

Thumar continued backing away from the angels, leaving Putnah to fight the battle alone."

"We are mightier than they!" He shouted at Putnah. "We must defend what is rightfully ours. The human belongs to us!"

Putnah lunged at the warrior standing closest to him. He had hoped that by eliminating one, Thumar would take on the other. The last thing Putnah would ever see was Thumar exiting through the basement ceiling.

Dear friends, do not be surprised at the painful trial you are suffering, as though something strange were happening to you.
—1 Peter 4:12 (NIV)

We are twice armed if we fight with faith.
—Plato

Chapter Xx

Samara brought up the contact list on her Blackberry. Enough was enough. It was time to call in the troops. What she needed was a good old-fashioned pajama party. Max had finally quieted down. He lay at her feet, watching the basement door.

She was still sitting at the kitchen table when her first guests rang the bell. Max retired to his favorite bedroom.

"Sam," it was Lu, with her husband Charlie in tow, "you know better than to be sitting over here scared to death all by yourself. I swear."

"I know." Samara hugged her faithful friends. "Please don't fuss. It's been a really long day."

Lourdes dropped her overnight bag in the foyer and headed straight for the kitchen. She was already in her robe and slippers.

"Charlie's gonna check the house." Lu shouted over her shoulder. "I told him about the basement door being unlocked."

"Thanks Charlie." Samara was grateful. "I'm probably being ridiculous, but the whole thing was just so creepy."

"It's most likely nothing to worry about." He ambled down the basement steps. "The door's probably been unlocked for a while and nobody knew. I checked around the back before we came in. Everything looks okay. I'll just make a quick sweep and get out of you girls' way."

"I brought three different kinds of ice cream." Lu was still talking. "Steph is bringing the snacks, and Celeste said she'll stop by the all-night place and pick up some sandwiches."

By the time the others arrived, Charlie had checked the entire house from top to bottom.

"You ladies are safe and sound." He said. "Set the alarm as soon as I shut the door. I'm leaving Max in charge."

He grabbed a few sandwiches off the tray, kissed his wife, and stood outside on the porch until he heard the door lock and the alarm engage. Lourdes blew her husband another kiss through the closed window.

Samara made a fresh pot of gourmet coffee while the girls set the table in the dining room. Lu pulled out the china and crystal. Stephanie and Celeste prepared the food. Getting together was a special occasion and they were doing it up right. When everything was ready, they all sat at the big table and joined hands.

"Father," Celeste prayed for the group, "You have connected our lives in a way that only You could. Thank you for the gift of friendship. We pray for our Nana Anna and ask that you strengthen her, even while she rests. She is Sam's grandmother, but she has loved all of us just like we were family. Her home has always been open to us. She has never been too busy to lend an ear or heat up a slice of homemade pie. We also pray for our friend Sam. She has endured through some very difficult times. We ask that You give her the courage to keep going. Let our coming together be a reminder of how much she is loved."

"And Lord," Stephanie took the prayer up a notch, "We take authority over any and every demonic influence that would seek to harm our sister. This house is off-limits to Satan and his henchmen. We declare that no weapon forged against Sam will prevail. She belongs to You, and You are the Greater One. You promised us that if we submit ourselves to You and resist Satan that he must flee. In Jesus' name, we pray with thanksgiving. Amen."

Everyone said amen, but no one opened her eyes. Neither did they break the circle. An indescribably wonderful peace filled the house and settled over the women. Their heads remained bowed as they basked in the serenity of the moment. It was not to be rushed.

Had they opened their eyes a few moments earlier, they might have witnessed a brilliant flash of lightning through the crack at the bottom of the basement door; or discerned the presence of the guardians hovering directly above them.

When the moment had passed, they all lifted their heads as if on cue. Samara broke the silence.

"I can't begin to thank you all for being here." She spoke warmly as she dabbed her eyes with one of the napkins on the table. "To think that you'd drop everything to come and stay with me is so humbling. I love you guys so much."

"We love you too." Each woman responded.

"Okay, enough of the mushy stuff. Let's eat." Lu scooped up a sandwich. "I'm hungry all of a sudden."

"You're always hungry," Celeste retorted.

Samara smiled at her houseguests. The friendly banter was somehow comforting. She couldn't imagine her life without these women. They were more than just friends. This was her extended family sitting at the table in their favorite pajamas snacking on goodies.

"Guess who called me?" She asked nonchalantly.

"Who?" Lu managed before chomping down on another buffalo wing.

"Tony."

Everyone stopped mid-chew. Samara picked a sandwich from the stack. Lu placed the half-eaten chicken on her plate.

"I know you don't think you're gonna just drop a bomb like that and then pick up a sandwich?" She insisted.

"Not hardly," Celeste chimed in. "Out with it girl."

"Yeah, spill it," Stephanie said. "We want all the juicy details, and don't leave anything out."

Samara looked around the table. If she could trust anybody with her deepest secrets, it was these women. Each one would take the information to her grave. It would go no farther than that house. They stared back at her, waiting.

"Well," Samara began, "I was minding my own business at the hospital when I got this call from an unknown number. At first I wasn't going to answer it, but I guess I wanted to know who had my number when I didn't have theirs."

"What did you do when you heard his voice?" Celeste wanted to get to the good stuff.

"I froze. I mean, I literally couldn't think."

"What did he want, and how did he get your number?" Stephanie asked.

"His mom gave it to him. He said he wants to get together to talk about the kids."

"Did you say get together, as in meet somewhere?" Lu was nonplused.

"Yep."

"And are you?" Celeste pushed harder.

"I wasn't. But my dad told me I'd be holding the kids hostage if I didn't."

"That's deep." Celeste responded. "It's true too, when you think about it. They shouldn't have to choose sides."

"They must miss Tony something terrible." Stephanie added. "I can't imagine not being able to see my dad. We're so close."

"I hadn't really thought about it like that before." Samara confessed. "In my mind Tony didn't deserve to see them. I guess that doesn't change the fact that he is their dad. My stepfather is the only dad I have ever known. I'm grateful for everything he's done and the difference he's made in my life."

"So let's get down to the nitty and the gritty." Lu was ready to move on. "How do you feel about seeing Tony again? And be honest. We can handle it."

Samara sat back in the chair. The girls were right; it was time for her to come clean. Hearing Tony's voice again had awakened something that honestly scared her. She wasn't sure what it was, but it was freaking her out.

"A part of me wants to go just so I can show him what he left behind. On the other hand, I want to put as much distance as possible between me and my past. I'm afraid that if I see him, it's gonna take me right back to a place I don't ever want to be again."

The women sat in reflective silence, sipping on their coffee. Each one quietly contemplated what she would do if she were in Samara's shoes. Lu was the first to speak.

"We will support whichever decision you make, mama. If you decide to go, we will all go with you if you need us to. Right, ladies?"

"Right!" They sang out in unison.

"By the way," Stephanie inquired, "where is this meeting supposed to take place?"

Samara put forth her best poker face. She retrieved her sandwich and began spreading mustard on the bread.

"His place." She answered without looking up.

"Uh–huh." Somebody whispered.

Her sister-friends eyed each other knowingly across the table. Samara finished spreading the mustard and reached for the pickles. This was going to be one crazy night.

*I have fought the good fight. I have finished
the race. I have kept the faith.*
—2 Timothy 4:7 (NIV)

CHAPTER XXI

JABNIEL OCCUPIED THE CHAIR in the corner of the hospital room. His subject had not yet regained consciousness, but was resting peacefully. As far as the doctors could determine, her vital signs were stable, albeit weak. Jabniel knew better. Anna Morton was alive and well; she was keenly aware of his presence.

This was a glorious day. He would soon deliver her soul into the presence of the Almighty, where her reward awaited her. She had fought a good fight and had advanced into the final stages of the transition. It would not be much longer now. Gabriel had sent word by another messenger that he was to wait for the command.

Jabniel arose from his chair at the appearance of his commander.

"Prince Michael." He saluted the archangel.

"This is a faithful soldier." Michael looked upon Anna's radiant face. "Her time is at hand, and she is not afraid."

"I have been communicating with her in the altered state. She is indeed ready." Jabniel reported.

"So she is, but there is one more assignment that she must complete." Michael instructed. "The granddaughter is to receive her blessing. Lariel will escort her here tomorrow. I have ordered additional forces posted throughout the area."

The archangel moved to where Anna lay sleeping. He extended his wings, completely engulfing the hospital bed. Brilliant light flooded the room as he looked toward the heavens. Doctors and nurses scurried up and down the hall without ever noticing the glorious ceremony that was taking place right under their noses.

"Faithful servant, you are called from labor to rest." The Archangel touched her forehead. "We bestow upon you this final duty."

* * *

"Hey, Nana."

"There's my sweet pea. Didn't think I'd see you so early this morning." Anna reached for the remote and raised her bed to sitting position. "The nurse told me you were here until late last night."

"I didn't want to leave, but the doctor said you'd probably sleep through the night. Mom promised to stay with you. She called and told me that you had awakened."

Samara dragged the visitor's chair closer to her grandmother and planted a kiss on her forehead.

"Your mom slept in the recliner. Her face was the first thing I saw when I woke up." Anna shifted a little. "Most of our conversation was about you. She loves you very much, you know."

"I know she does." Samara twirled a loose strand of hair between her fingers. "We just don't see eye to eye on things. She thinks she is entitled to have the last word on everything from where I should be living to how I am raising my children. Nothing I do is ever good enough for her."

"She wants what's best for you and the kids. You can't blame her for that."

"I'm not saying that she can't express her opinions; but what's best for my family is for me to decide, not her. Why can't she let me live my own life, and offer a little encouragement every now and then? That's not asking too much."

"You know how difficult it is to sit back and watch your children suffer. Mothers are the worst. We can't help ourselves." Anna squeezed her granddaughter's hand with what little strength she could muster. "Give your mom a chance. Would you do that for me?"

Samara thought about her own children. It hurt. She longed for the chance to sit and talk with them—to laugh again. Maybe she was more like her mother than she dared believe. It was time to break the ridiculous cycle.

"Okay, Nana." She gave in. "I don't know how much good it'll do, but I owe it to the kids to at least try."

"Promise?" Anna persisted.

"I promise."

Samara unfolded the white blanket at the foot of the hospital bed and spread it over her grandmother. She grimaced at the protruding intravenous needles and fought back the gathering tears. This was not the time for pity. Her grandmother needed to have this conversation, and she would have to handle it like a grown woman. How many times had she cried on her nana's shoulder? It was her turn to listen now.

"How did you sleep last night?" Anna broke the heavy silence. "It was your first night in the big house without me."

"Not too bad. The girls came over and stayed with me. They send their love." Samara surveyed the hospital room. "Who brought the flowers?"

"Pastor Bromley dropped them off early this morning. We had a pleasant little visit. He prayed with me and your mom."

"That was nice." Samara hesitated. "Did he mention anything about our meeting?"

"Not really. He asked about you though," Anna threw in, as if an afterthought.

"What exactly did he say?" Samara looked down at her feet, displaying a sudden interest in the laces on her boots.

"My goodness," Anna feigned exasperation, "I feel like the matchmaker in the middle of everything, and all, and whatnot. Maybe the two of you should be asking the questions person-to-person."

"Hardly—I was just curious. That's not the same as being interested." Samara quickly changed the subject. "Anyway, there were quite a few calls for you at the house."

"It's nice to be remembered." Anna glanced at the flowers sitting on the window ledge. "You know, baby girl, just this morning I was thinking about the splendidness of God's nature. You ever notice how many beautiful shades and colors of roses you can buy these days? The pastels are so pretty. There's even a green one in that bunch Pastor Bromley gave me."

"So I see." Samara smiled.

"But I noticed something else," her grandmother pressed on, "As beautiful as they are, I didn't smell anything when your mom held them to my nose. And they don't have any thorns on them either. Pastor said that they're the new hybrids."

"If we can clone animals then I guess I shouldn't be too surprised that it can be done with flowers." Samara wrinkled her nose. "Seems like waste to me. Why have flowers if you can't smell them?"

"Real roses smell so good, don't they?'

"They do." Samara knew her grandmother was getting at something.

The room became very still. For those few precious moments, nothing mattered except the two of them. Even the sound of the beeping monitors faded into the background.

"Your nana's tired, Sweet Pea." Anna's eyes clouded over as she looked past Samara. "I want to go home."

"I know." Samara rose from the chair and sat on the side of the bed. "I'm going to get you out of here as soon as the doctor says you can go."

"I want to see my mother and father, my sisters, and my Robbie."

In that bittersweet moment, Samara resigned to the truth she already knew. Her nana had come to terms with what God had allowed. She looked so peaceful.

"I'm trying not to be selfish, Nana, but what would I do without you? Nobody else gets me."

"Just keep living honey. Put one foot in front of the other. Remember, the Bible says that the Lord directs our steps."

"If God is really orchestrating my every move, then He and I need to have a talk."

"Things only appear confusing because we can't see everything going on behind the scenes. Yet, He has seen fit to give you a little glimpse. That's what your dreams are about. Wouldn't you say?"

"I don't know.' Samara looked in her grandmother's face. "Do you really think God is trying to show me something?"

"He's not trying, honey. He's done it."

Samara considered what she knew about the God of the Bible. It didn't seem likely that an all-powerful, all-knowing Deity would spend His precious time divulging some heretofore-unknown secret to a disenchanted, confused human. She wasn't saying it was impossible, but definitely seemed most improbable. There had to be a more deserving candidate. Yet, she could not deny that what her grandmother had said resonated deep within. Maybe the talks with Noah were really paying off.

"I've been reading those books that Noah gave me. There is so much information, I feel overwhelmed. I'm trying to make the connection between where I am, and where this is headed. You know more about these things than I do. What do you think it means?" Samara pleaded.

"He has chosen to reveal something to you that most of us have never, and perhaps will never see until we get to heaven.

There is a reason why that demon in your dreams is trying to scare you. He's trying to frustrate the purpose of God."

"But what am I supposed to do if I don't understand what that purpose is? I can't very well call God on the telephone and have a little chat."

"You don't have to have all the answers right now. Just settle it within yourself that this is happening and that God has predestined you to be the candidate for the job. It's His call, dear."

"But that's just it; I don't know what I'm giving in to. I'm still trying to figure out how to make my own life work. In case He hasn't noticed, I haven't done so well in the 'making good choices' category."

"Just rest in the truth of His love for you, and that He knows what you can and cannot handle. When it's time for you to know more, He will reveal it."

"It seems to me that God would choose someone less spastic. How can you be so sure, Nana?"

"My dear Sweet Pea," Anna smiled at her favorite grandchild, "the pieces of the puzzle will come together. He would not show you something and then tell you to figure it out for yourself. The answer is hidden in plain sight. Perhaps you should start by forgiving yourself—and Tony. The Father has sent His angels to help you. You can do this honey."

Samara offered a cautious smile. "I don't have the strength to forgive. I'm not ready to let him off the hook."

"All things in His time honey, not ours. You will be okay. You're much stronger than you think you are."

At that moment, Samara did not feel very strong. What little virtue she had was because of her grandmother. This woman loved her unconditionally, and allowed her the space to be herself. Not once did she exhibit the slightest hint of judgment or condemnation. If God were to take her now, it would be the last straw.

"Trust me, it will all make sense." Anna placed her needle-infused hand on Samara's. Remember what I said about the flowers?"

"Yes. You can tell the real from the fake by the aroma."

This time, Samara let the tears roll silently down her face and fall onto her grandmother's blanket.

"And never forget," Anna's hand trembled slightly as she gently patted her granddaughter's face, "real roses have thorns."

"I love you, Nana." She didn't bother wiping her tears.

"I love you too, Sweet Pea." Anna smiled the smile of a woman at peace with herself and with her God.

For if you forgive men when they sin against you, your heavenly Father will also forgive you. But if you do not forgive men their sins, your Father will not forgive your sins.
—*Matthew 6:14–15(NIV)*

Chapter XXII

Samara had been sitting in her car for almost an hour. She was not stuck in traffic this time. In fact, she was still in the driveway of her grandmother's house. Had she done what normal people do, she would have turned the engine over and been on her way.

She was not sure why she had agreed to meet Tony at his place. There was no reason why they could not discuss the kids over the phone. No good thing could possibly come out of meeting face-to-face.

She strategically positioned the Blackberry in the passenger seat next to her pocketbook. All she had to do was send a text message and cancel the whole thing: No harm, no foul. However, if her mother was right, and she is always right, then this should be a drama-free event. This was strictly about the kids. Everything else was behind them. The damage could not be reversed. That is, of course, if Samara was really through with him.

She knew better, but she could not help but blame herself for her failed marriage and the breakdown of her family. The right woman would have made him stay. Maybe if she had been smarter, prettier, funnier, taller, shorter, heavier or thinner. And now she was in the prime of her life, and she was alone. She was not supposed to be by herself. Not now. Not after all she had given.

After Tony left, her girlfriends had come together to comfort her, the way girlfriends do. They unanimously agreed that none of it was her fault and tried desperately to get her to see it their way.

"He had major issues." They had sucked their teeth in unified disgust. "It's totally his loss. You're better off without him."

They were her friends and they loved her, but Samara knew better. Bottom line, they still had their perfect little lives. Whether married or single, they were each in a good place, and would not dare trade with her. She had failed the "good little Christian wife" test.

The ex-husband and father of her children had stopped contributing to the household expenses the day he moved out. He didn't bother telling her that he was cutting them off. The money in their joint account simply disappeared.

Samara swore she would not ask him for help, but after a few months, she had no choice. It was too much to carry alone. She swallowed her pride and called his job, only to be told that he had taken an extended leave of absence. They were not exactly sure when he'd be back.

The receptionist asked if she wanted to leave a message for when he returned, but she didn't bother responding. Instead, she banged the phone down onto the receiver, multiple times. She had hoped the receptionist did not take it personally, but she was not about to leave her name. That bit of gossip would have spread through the office like wildfire.

Tony had managed to disappear off the face of the earth. He had a knack for getting lost when he wanted to. The CIA would have been hard pressed to find him. After much finagling, Samara was able to gather information through the old reliable grapevine. There was always somebody willing to give up the goods. It only cost a pound of flesh and a large slice of dignity.

As it turned out, Tony was staying with some family members in the Midwest. Samara was barely on life support by the time she tracked them down. It did not help. They were not about to squeal on their cousin, but said they would get the message to him if they happened to hear from him. She knew what that meant—don't hold your breath.

By the time he had resurfaced, it was too late to save the house. The payments were too far behind, and Samara had already remortgaged the loan, twice. She could not sell it without his approval. The bank had extended all the grace there was to be had.

Before the great demise, Samara had managed her money like a pro. Her healthy savings, vacation, and Christmas club accounts were direct results of her parent's teaching on the benefits of credit worthiness. Work hard, pay your bills on time, and save as much as possible, they said. It was no easy feat but

Samara prided herself on having done just that. She had built a nice little nest egg for her family.

None of that mattered anymore. The stuff showing up on her credit report was downright embarrassing. The foreclosure alone was enough to seal her financial future for the next nine years, minimum. She was sure that her face was posted in the annals of every credit scoring company known to man. No need worrying about identity theft. Any self-respecting thief would leave her be, or at least try to sell her somebody *else's* history.

Samara needed to quiet the alarm sounding off in her head. All she had to her name was her 401K account, and the benefits package her company had given her when they gave her the boot. She had been caught in the crosshairs of a major re-org. Some brilliantine at the top thought it was cheaper to lay off the higher salaried employees and replace them with less knowledgeable, less expensive job seekers. That was the last time she would leave her future in the hands of some senior executive who cared more about the bottom line than about their dedicated workers.

"Whatever," Samara released a frustrated breath.

She turned the key in the ignition. It was time to go meet the man. As she backed out of the driveway, a strange premonition came over her. Chills ran down her spine as she remembered that she had done this before. It was the same as in the dream. She did not know what to make of it.

Now she was nervous.

If he sins against you seven times in a day, and seven times comes back to you and says, "I repent," forgive him.
—Luke 17:4 (NIV)

Chapter XXIII

Tony peeked out his living room window, being careful not to move the drapes too far back. The last thing he wanted was for her to catch him looking. His mother had convinced him to call the kids, but there was no way he would do that without talking with Samara first. He owed her that much.

He released the curtain and resumed his stance in front of the television. His ex-wife was true to form. Her proclivity for showing up late still irritated him. If anything good could be said about him, he was a stickler for being prompt. It was a left over from his stint in the military.

Samara had chosen the time, but she was still late. He would have to wait. No matter—it gave him a chance to rehearse his story. He only hoped to say it without the whole thing turning into an ugly mess.

Tony shook his head, dislodging the unpleasant thoughts permanently wedged in his memory. There was a time when life was not so complicated. He had it all—a beautiful wife, three wonderful children, a good job, a beautiful home, and one dog of questionable pedigree. It was everything a man could ask for. They were living the American dream. He should have been satisfied.

The only problem was that he also had an addiction. He never talked about the habit to anyone. It was a little something he had picked up when he was a teen. His best friend had stumbled upon some magazines hidden in their garage. They spent many a day flipping through the pages when the parents weren't home. Eventually they graduated to cruising adults sites on the computer. There was no turning back. Tony was hooked.

When he met Samara, he was sure that his love for her would cure him of the dreadful obsession. He was happy with his life, was able to stay away from the adult sites for several years. Deliverance had come at last, he thought.

He never told her about his struggle. There was no need. The dirty little habit was a part of his past. His family was his future. It was over, and that was that. At least, that is what he told himself—until it began to unravel. The habit that he thought was under control reared its ugly head unannounced and with a vengeance. It kicked the door in and steamrolled its way back.

To this day, he could not remember how he ended up on that site. But there it was, staring back at him, taunting him. He had to make a decision immediately. Shut it down, or scroll to the next page. He chose the latter.

Just when he thought, *I have mastered this*; it rose up and mastered him. He would be okay for a few weeks. Then, without warning, he would fall head long in to the same predicted pattern. It wasn't even satisfying any more. He couldn't even explain why he was doing it. He felt dirty when he indulged, and guilty when he didn't. The juice wasn't worth the squeeze.

He had ignored the warning signs, spending more and more time on the websites and in the chat rooms. He even indulged at work. If his boss ever found out, he would be fired for sure. The addiction was way out of control. His world came crashing down too fast to recover. He was blindsided.

Someone had made an invoicing mistake and mailed the bill for his "adult" phone calls to the house. He had signed up to pay on line, but the invoice landed on his dining room table, mixed in with the other bills. Of course, Samara was the one to discover it. At least it wasn't one of the kids. Exposing his family to the madness was worse than the act itself. He loved them too much for that.

Tony pulled the curtains back again, wondering if this was really a good idea. Maybe Samara was standing him up on purpose. He couldn't blame her. It would cost him a couple of hours, but at least he wouldn't be spending the entire night alone. Some of the guys from the job were picking him up later. They were going to the sports bar across town to shoot a little pool. The Bible study group at work sponsored the outing.

He didn't belong to the study group, but he loved pool. The whole religious thing turned him off. He knew the Bible for himself, please and thank you. His mother had raised him in the church. They practiced family devotions until the day he left for college. The Christian walk had been a way of life.

Samara had been a regular churchgoer when they met. There was always something going on at her church, and she was faithful in her attendance. After they were married, she had dragged him to practically every service. She had signed them both up to be youth advisors until the kids got older.

Tony had had enough. What others ate did not make him fat. The whole church thing left him empty and unfulfilled. The way he figured it, if God really loved him, He would not have let some irresponsible drunk driver take his son's life.

If you forgive anyone his sins, they are forgiven; if you do not forgive them, they are not forgiven.
—John 20:23 (NIV)

Chapter XXIV

"Thanks for coming," Tony greeted her at the door.

Samara offered no response other than nodding her head. She entered the apartment and waited for him to lead the way.

"We can sit in here." He escorted her to the living room. "Can I get you something? I have bottled water."

"No." She seemed uncomfortable. "I'm good."

"Have a seat, please." Tony offered.

Samara sat on the edge of the old sofa, her back perfectly straight. She placed her pocketbook on her lap and clasped hands together. In a matter of seconds, she had assessed everything within viewing range, except Tony. They had yet to look each other in the eye for longer than two consecutive seconds.

Tony crossed the room and sat in the chair strategically positioned so as not to invade each other's space. He had anticipated some degree of tension, but not the nervousness boiling in his stomach. Seeing her again had jump-started a range of emotions he thought he had squashed. The woman had not aged one bit. She looked amazing.

He grabbed the remote and muted the television. The stall tactic would give him enough time to settle his mind. The two of them stared at the screen as the local news report streamed in closed-captions.

"So, how are things?"

He regretted asking the question almost as soon as the words fell from his lips. It was a stupid way to begin the conversation.

"As well as can be expected," Samara answered without turning from the television.

Tony did not miss the inference. He had prepared for the worst.

"I'm sorry to hear about your grandmother." He moved past the deliberate insult. "She's one of the nicest people I know."

"Yes she is."

"Please let her know that I asked for her."

They stared at the muted television in awkward silence for several agonizing seconds.

"What do you want from me Tony?" Samara faced him for the first time. "Why am I here?"

Tony searched the eyes of the woman he had deserted. She was his first love and the mother of his children. He wanted, needed to tell her how sorry he was: Sorry for walking out, sorry for dumping everything on her, sorry that their son was gone. There was just no way to do that without sounding trite and lame. It was too late in the game for apologies. They would have to get past this.

"I asked you to come because I want to talk about the kids."
He pressed on: "Not a day goes by that I don't regret leaving
them. My mom brings me pictures and keeps me updated, but
it doesn't fill the void."

"So I'm supposed to feel sorry for you?" Samara's voice
was rising. "You've been AWOL for the last three years of your
children's lives! I should get an Oscar for managing to convince
them that their father really does love them; that he just needs
a little time to get himself together."

"I'm not asking for your pity, Sam."

"Then what do you want? Am I supposed to give you my
blessing because you are ready to be a father again? "

"That's not fair. You know why I left. My life was out of
control and I did not want to take my family down that road.
Do I have to get your okay to see my own children because of
that?"

"You want to talk about fair?" She was mad now. "Fair is
when you help pay the bills because your *own* children need
a place to live. Fair is calling your *own* children and assuring
them that this had nothing to do with them. It's showing up
when they graduate from high school or just need some fatherly
advice. Or how about calling them on their birthdays?"

Samara stopped talking. She looked away so that Tony
would not see the tears. He didn't have to. After twenty-five
years of marriage, he knew her like no one else did. She was
angry and had every right to be.

He had finally come face-to-face with the full consequences
of his addiction. Up until now, he had done a good job keeping
the guilt and the shame in check. He had convinced himself

that the kids were better off without him. But they did not have the luxury of denial.

"Listen Sam, I can't even begin to imagine what these past three years must've been like for you and the kids."

"No you can't."

"Please hear me out." Tony forged on. "I can't bring that time back. But I can rebuild on what was once a very solid foundation. I love my children and I intend to be a part of their lives again. I know I could have contacted them on my own, and leave you out of the loop. They are practically adults. I just thought it would be better if we approached this together. It would make it easier for them."

"Easier for them, or for you?"

"I deserve that, but I'm not backing down on this, Sam."

The doorbell rang, startling them both.

"Excuse me." Tony headed down the narrow hallway." I am supposed to be shooting some pool tonight. The guys must be early."

He opened the door without checking the peephole.

"Hey." He was unpleasantly surprised. "What's up?"

"Are you going to let me in, or do we do this out here?" The voice asked.

Tony gave his uninvited guest the blank stare of a man caught in a difficult situation. It was worse than a raccoon in headlights. He could see Samara out of the corner of his eye gathering her things. She had gotten up from the couch and was preparing to leave. He needed her to stay so that they could work this through. There was no way that was going to happen now.

"You know this isn't a good time." He pleaded. "I told you it would be about an hour."

"And I told you that I wanted to meet her." She pushed him out of the way. "Let me in, Tony."

Ilana Peterson entered the arena, making a beeline for the living room. She did not wait to be escorted. Tony made a failed attempt to get there first, but Ilana was not allowing any interference. Samara was standing ringside by the time they both hit the ropes.

"Samara, this is Ilana Peterson." Tony extended the superfluous introduction.

"I was just leaving." Samara spoke directly to Tony.

He understood. She was not about to accommodate the girlfriend. She didn't have to. He regretted telling Ilana that they were meeting. She had said that she was okay with it, and even encouraged him when he'd had second thoughts. Now she was forcing Samara to deal with her. He resented the intrusion.

"Please don't leave on my account." Ilana wasted no time. "I can make myself comfortable in the other room."

Both women were clear on their positions.

"I'll see you to the door." Tony led the way of escape.

"Nice meeting you," Ilana added as she plopped on the sofa.

Tony knew that he had to say something—anything. It had taken him this long to face his past. He was not going down again without a fight. His children were worth it.

"I'm really sorry." He opened the door. "Believe it or not, this was a total surprise. Would it be okay if I called you later?"

"Don't bother." Samara barely spoke above a whisper.

He watched her walk down the steps and through the main doors. She never looked back.

When I was a child, I talked like a child, I thought like a child, I reasoned like a child. When I became a man, I put childish ways behind me.
—*1 Corinthians 13:11 (NIV)*

Chapter Xxv

"Hi, honey. Where are you?"

"I'm at home. What's wrong?"

"Are you by yourself?" Elinor still had not answered her daughter.

"Mom, what's wrong?" Samara already knew. "Is it Nana?"

Elinor just could not say it. She could not say that her mother was dead.

"It's okay sweetheart." Elinor spoke tenderly. "She was ready."

"I know. The last time I saw her she was trying to say goodbye. I guess I wasn't ready to hear it. No matter how sick she was, she had always managed to fight back. Going home was what kept her motivated. It was different this time."

Samara began to cry. Her beloved nana was gone. She was not coming home ever again.

"She was waiting for me to release her too," Elinor wept quietly, "but I just couldn't. I know it's selfish, but I could not imagine my life without her. She has always been there. Thank God for your father. He prayed and asked God to help me let her go."

It was the first tender moment that Samara and her mother had shared in years.

"I love you sweetheart."

"I love you too, Mom."

Elinor handed the phone to her husband.

"Are you okay, Sam?"

"I don't know."

"I'm sending Tony to get you." He instructed. "I know you guys haven't ironed out the kinks yet, but you'll have to put that aside for now. The family needs to be together. Just go straight to the house. Your mother and I will take care of things here. Lu and Charlie are picking up the kids."

"Okay, Dad. Thanks. I love you"

"I love you too. You know that."

Right then Samara loved her stepdad more than she ever had before. He was the anchor the family needed at that very moment. His was the voice of calm reassurance. She didn't have the strength to resist his decision to call Tony. This was not the time. Their issues did not seem so important anymore. Maybe she would give him the opportunity to finish their conversation after all.

Samara placed the phone on its cradle and climbed the stairs to her grandmother's room. The house settled into a heavy silence. She stood at the entranceway. Max was lying across the bed as if he knew somehow. He did not lift his head or wag his tail the way he usually did.

Everything was neat and tidy, just as her nana had left it that Sunday. She could still feel her presence, as if her grandmother were there, but in some unseen place. Samara entered the room and sat on the floor. An hour passed before either she or Max made a sound or moved from their places.

Tony rang the bell just as Samara was coming back down the stairs.

"Hi." He remained outside on the porch. "I'm so sorry about Nana Anna. I know how much you loved her. We all did."

"Thanks." Samantha didn't have much else to say. "I'll be right out."

She grabbed her things. Once again, life was happening and she was on the stage playing her part. But this time, she had been invited to the rehearsals. The scenes were unfolding right before her very eyes. It was beginning to make sense, although she could not articulate it yet. Something was stirring deep down inside.

"I hope you don't mind my going to your parents." Tony said. "When your father called with the news, the first thing I thought about was you in the big house all by yourself. It just seemed right for me to come. Your grandmother was one of my favorite people."

"It's okay, Tony." Her smile was sad but sincere. "Nana loved you like she loved the rest of us. You are family. She would want you to be here. That's what matters."

Samara gave herself permission let it go. She was not going to waste another minute of her life thinking up ways to make Tony suffer for what he had done. That was between him and his God. She would not stand in the way of him reconnecting with the kids. The brevity of life and the reality of death weighed in the balance.

She thought about the dream she'd had about her biological father. It had never dawned on her that she had been carrying the dead weight of a lost relationship. She did not want that to happen to her children. Her stepdad was right. They needed their father.

"Thanks, Sam." Tony returned the smile. "That means a lot coming from you. I know there is no way I can undo the wrong I have done, and I wouldn't blame you if you never forgave me. But please believe that our children mean the world to me. I'm thankful for this miracle of a second chance."

"You might think that this is just about the kids, but your second chance is more about you," she said. "You've been given another opportunity to get it right."

Samara gazed through the car window. People were going about their everyday business, but her world had changed in an instant. Just then, images from the dream resurfaced in rapid motion. She had an epiphany. This was about saving Tony's soul. Her nana's passing had set off an irrevocable chain of events.

*Go home to your family and tell them how much the Lord
has done for you, and how he has had mercy on you.*
—*Mark 5:19b (NIV)*

Chapter XXVI

THE HOUSE WAS FULL by the time Tony and Samara arrived. They let themselves in using Samara's key. People were everywhere. Their daughter was the first to see them. She met them at the door.

"I can't believe she's gone." Deborah hugged her mother.

"I know, honey." Samara said. "But Nana's not suffering anymore. She would not want to come back from her place in heaven either. Don't you worry; we'll see her again."

Tony stood next to them, looking a little uncomfortable. He didn't know what to expect. Deborah turned to him and fell into his arms.

"Daddy." She was his little girl again. "Mom-Mom told us you were coming. I've been watching the door all night, hoping you didn't change your mind."

"And miss seeing my baby girl?"

Tony held his daughter for a long time. Samara walked away so that they could have a moment. She was proud of her daughter. Deborah displayed an unconditional forgiveness that instantly put Tony at ease. There were no explanations needed. They would have plenty of time for that later.

She headed toward the kitchen where her mother was sure to be slicing and dicing one of the many hams, chickens, or cakes dropped off by caring folks. The next-door neighbor stopped her on the way.

"My goodness, Samara, it's so good to see you. You're looking more and more like your mother every day."

"Yes, Mrs. Harriett, it's good to see you too." Samara gave her Oscar winning smile.

Mrs. Harriett was not the person you wanted to run into if you were in a hurry. Before long, she would be pulling out pictures of her great-grandchildren, and giving blow-by-blow accounts of their every pubescent moment. Samara was preparing her getaway speech, when someone touched her elbow.

"Hey. I wanted to speak before heading out." It was Noah. "Would you excuse us, Mrs. Harriett?"

"Why certainly, dears." The nice neighbor peered over the rim of her glasses at the handsome couple.

"Where did you come from?" Samara asked. "I didn't realize you were here."

"Your mother called the church. I was able to make it to the hospital right before your grandmother passed away. If it helps, she looked beautiful. She was truly at peace."

"Thank you, Noah. That helps more than you know."

They were silent for a reflective moment.

"Well," Noah hesitated, "I'm going to head on out. I wanted to pray with the family and offer the services of the church.

Your grandmother was a long-standing member. Just let us know what you need us to do."

"My mom will be handling most of the details."

"Actually, she said she'd be bringing you with her tomorrow to make the final arrangements. She said your grandmother wanted it that way."

"Oh." Samara was surprised. "I guess I'll see you tomorrow then."

They faced each other, feeling suddenly awkward.

"Well, Reverend." Mrs. Harriett came to the rescue. "It was certainly good seeing you. I must be leaving as well."

She hugged Noah and Samara, and then she faced them toward each other, singlehandedly forcing the connection. They practically collided in their embrace.

It had been a while since Samara felt the strong arms of a man around her. A hint of his cologne filtered through her nose. She had forgotten what that was like. It was nice.

"There now," Mrs. Harriett smiled. "That wasn't so bad, was it?"

"Not at all," said Noah, finding his voice. "I'll walk you out, Mrs. Harriett. Good night, Samara."

"Good night."

Samara watched them as they made their way to the door. She also caught the eye of her ex-husband, who had not missed one second of the encounter.

Elinor surfaced from the kitchen. Her eyes were still red from crying, but she was forever the consummate host. She had learned from the best. Anna Morton would have it no other way.

"Samara, you're here." Elinor embraced her.

"Yes I am. Need any help?"

"No dear. You know me. I have to stay busy. It's my way of coping."

"Have you seen Nicky?" Samara looked around.

"He's downstairs with the rest of the young people. They're playing those video games with your dad."

"I appreciate everything Dad has done. He really is amazing."

"That's why I married him. He's the best thing that ever happened to me; after you and the kids, of course." Elinor touched Samara's hand.

"Oh, Mom." Samara choked back the tears. "It's just us now. Nana was the last of her generation."

"And we're going to do them proud because they taught us well. We are their legacy. Just look around you. Everybody is here. The circle has not been broken."

Samara surveyed the house. Aunts, uncles, cousins, neighbors, and friends moved about, sharing their stories of the woman who had touched so many lives. Classic hymns of faith played softly in the background. Somebody yelled out from the game room. The incessant melody of life saturated the premises, reassuring its inhabitants that everything was going to be okay.

Elinor placed a sealed envelope in Samara's hand.

"What is this?" Samara asked.

She recognized her grandmother's handwriting.

"It's for you, from Mom." Elinor kissed her on her forehead. "But don't open it here. Wait until you get home. That's the way she wanted it."

If Satan drives out Satan, he is divided against himself. How then can his kingdom stand?
—Matthew 12:26 (NIV)

Chapter XXVII

THIS WAS NOT GOING to fare well. Mastema had been summoned to a debriefing before the high council. If he survived the tribunal, he would have someone's head.

The old woman had died before they could extract anything from her. She had been the key to getting the girl. They had hoped to impart enough fear to render her useless. It should have been an easy victory, but the hag was always praying. She was out of their reach now. Her guardian had escorted her soul into the other dimension.

Now he would have to give an account as to why things were not going as planned. He should have destroyed Thumar long before this.

Mastema approached the throne.

"Master." The arch demon bowed low.

"It appears that your special project has taken an interesting turn of events." The superior commander's voice was calm and calculating. "My sources tell me that the enemy has increased its presence. The human has managed to reconnect with the spouse. This puts her directly where we did not want her.

The grandmother's death has set off a chain of events, further advancing the enemy's cause."

Mastema bristled at the suggestion that he was under-informed. He wondered who the secret "source" was.

"If I may speak, my lord?"

"We think you've done enough *speaking*. Have you determined a strategy? Or are we waiting to see what Michael has in mind?"

"I have my best soldiers on it. We will use the grandmother's death to our advantage."

"Continue ..."

"Now that the human has connected with the spouse," Mastema ventured, "we will re-introduce old fears and unresolved anger. I have assigned my best tormentors to lead the attack while she grieves for the grandmother. She will be too depressed to pursue The Word. We have also masterminded a new love interest. He will be used to distract our subject."

He waited for the verdict.

"Very well," the captain replied. "Do as you say. But know this, if your human survives unscathed once again, you will not see the light of another day. She is not to come into contact with Lariel again."

"I will not fail you, my lord."

Mastema relieved them of his presence. He would return to his domain and summon the soldiers responsible for reporting Thumar's whereabouts. They would find the ambitious traitor and destroy him.

He could not afford to trust his plan in the hands of his little minions. It was time to pay Lariel a personal visit.

See, I am doing anew thing! Now it springs up; do you not perceive it? I am making a way in the desert and streams in the wasteland.
—Isaiah 43:19 (NIV)

Chapter XXVIII

THE STACK OF LAUNDRY lay carefully folded in her chair. Her favorite sweat pants and tee shirt were on top, just as her nana had left them the last time she was there. Samara held the clothes to her chest and breathed in the fragrance. She would not cry. There would be no more wasted tears. She had devoted too much of her life to fear and self-loathing. Her nana was right. If she did not learn to be okay with her place in life, she would most likely spend the rest of it lonely and miserable.

Lu was downstairs fixing a sandwich. She was staying for a couple of nights while Charlie was out of town on business. Celeste and Stephanie would spend alternating nights throughout the week. The girls all had decided that Samara should not be left alone for the next week or so. She was finally starting to come around, and they intended to see to it that she stayed on the right road.

Samara sat on the edge of the bed, too tired to sleep. That was when she remembered the enveloped her mother had given her at the house. She retrieved it from her pocketbook and held it close to her heart. Seeing her grandmother's handwriting affected her in a way that was much unexpected. Breaking the seal was almost as traumatic. Every action served to finalize her nana's death.

She unfolded the document. The top page was a letter to her. It was dated several years earlier.

"My dear Sweet Pea,

When you get this letter, I will be in heaven with my dear Robbie and my beloved Jesus. What a glorious day. Try not to be too sad. I know you miss me because I am no longer with you in the flesh, but I will always be with you in spirit. Those times when it seems that the pain is too much to bear, just think about all of us being together in heaven for eternity. Won't that be grand? I can hardly wait.

You may be wondering what all this paperwork is about. The documents attached to this letter are the deeds to my house and to another piece of property in Virginia that belonged to my mother and father (your great-grandparents). Your grandfather and I always wanted you to have it. Everything is spelled out in my will. Your mother and father know all about it. They are the executors of my estate.

I did not tell you about this before because you would not have been able to receive it. You needed time to heal through your pain and disappointments. I believe by the spirit of God that when you get this, you will be ready. It is a lot to digest, so be sure to have the family attorney sit down with you. Your mom and dad will be able to help.

Do with this as you please. Nevertheless, whatever you decide to do, please do it for His glory. You will never go wrong.

I love you, Samara. You will always be my dearest sweet pea.

With much love,
Your Nana."

Samara stared at the letter, her eyes filling with tears. She read it over and over through blurred vision. It could not have been saying what she thought it was saying; but it was. The love that her nana had given her was a testament unto itself. Now, she had given her this incredible gift. Her heart ached for her grandmother. She needed to see her, to thank her.

Just a few months ago, Samara had been deep in the throes of foreclosure and bankruptcy. She had lost everything. Now, she would be receiving a lump sum of money, the deed to her grandmother's house, and some mystery property in Virginia. Her brain could not possibly begin to unpack that. Not tonight. It would have to wait until morning.

"Hey Sam!" Lu called her from the bottom of the stairs.

Samara padded to the hallway. What she needed was a good cup of coffee. She would not tell Lu about the deeds just yet. She would talk with her parents first.

"I'm coming. Hold your horses."

Samara turned at the top of the stairway to see a bewildered Lu holding a beautiful bouquet of roses.

"Wow. Where'd they come from?"

"The florist," Lu smirked. "Who's Matthew?"

*I will lie down and sleep in peace, for you alone,
O LORD, make me dwell in safety.*
—*Psalm 4:8 (NIV)*

Chapter Xxix

Several weeks had passed since the funeral. It was over. Noah had preached a beautiful eulogy for the woman whose life had spoken for her. Anna Morton was laid to rest.

The attorney had since reviewed the final paperwork for her grandmother's estate with Samara and her parents. The deeds to the properties would be transferred to her name. She was also a co-beneficiary on her grandmother's life insurance policy. Her grandparents had covered all their bases. Their legacy was intact.

Being in the house without Nana would take some getting used to. Lu was there again for a few days. She stayed over whenever Charlie was away. The house was big enough for them to move around in without bumping into each other. It was just good to know that someone else was around.

There were still moments when Samara expected to walk into the kitchen and see her grandmother standing over the stove. Some mornings she swore she smelled breakfast cooking.

She tied the fuzzy robe around her waist, basking in the bittersweet moment. Her laptop beckoned from across the room. This was a good time as any to add an entry to her new blog site. The thought of connecting with total strangers seemed a little weird, but it was time to throw caution to the wind. It would be the first baby step to breaking out of the self-imposed exile.

"This just might be fun, Max. There's nothing like connecting with folks as loony as you."

Samara laughed aloud for the first time in months. She sat Indian-style in the middle of her bed and turned the computer on. Suddenly, there was much to say.

Hey everybody. Welcome to my blog spot, "SagaCity." It is from the word *sagacity*, which means, "the quality of being sagacious," or "of keen and farsighted penetration and judgment: discerning."

Anyone who knows me will testify, anonymously of course, that my life has borne little resemblance to that of one who has lived a discerning lifestyle. Heretofore, my situation was a hot mess. From the outside looking in, it appeared that I had used neither sound judgment, nor levelheaded wisdom when making important life choices. In fact, one might suggest the total opposite.

Prior to this moment, that may have been an accurate observation. I just let life happen, not realizing that when you passively engage, life will do just that—happen.

I meandered through the maze that was my life, reacting to circumstances. Always reacting, waiting for the next scene to unfold. Know what I mean? Somewhere deep in my subconscious, I deduced that this is how it is. You simply submit to the vicissitudes of life, and hope for the best.

"Why is that?" you ask.

I think it began when I was a kid. My father died when I was still an infant. My mom ended up working two jobs to support the both of us. She could not do that without getting someone to watch me, so I spent the better part of my childhood in foster homes. I do not blame her. It was a sacrifice. She did what she thought was best.

Later on, I got married and had three beautiful children. We bought our dream house in the suburbs and settled in for the "happily ever after." Once again, life "happened." My oldest son died in a car accident, my spouse and I divorced, and we lost our home. Get the picture? Life just kept happening to me, and it seemed I had no control. So I buckled in and held on.

This may be too much information, but the end justifies the means. Keep reading.

Just when I had determined that this was my sad, pitiful lot, something else "happened." I started having weird dreams. Not only were they strange, but they were literally "out of this world." I could see things that apparently most of us cannot, or will not, see. It's like having authorized access to an invisible cosmos. The tricky part is that there seems to be a connection between this "other" place and our world, but we do not know it because we cannot see it.

Oh no, you're thinking, *I've pulled up some weirdo's blog.*

Do not sign off just yet. Hang in there with me. I am not suggesting that I was abducted by aliens, and have just recently returned. What I am proposing is that there is more to this life than what meets the eye—literally. Allow me to explain. Remember, the end justifies the means.

These dreams have a common thread—they all take place in an unseen dimension. I know, I'm sounding weird again. But not really. The Bible gives credibility to the existence of such things. It is the place where angels of light and darkness reside, and this place is very real. For some reason that I have yet to determine, I see it all in my dreams. (And no, I am not a Bible thumper. I am a believer).

Hence, the reason for my blog. I figure there is no way I am the only person in this great big world who has experienced such things. At this point, I am working on an I-need-to-know basis.

So here it is. If you have the slightest inkling of what I am talking about, hit me up. We will compare notes. Otherwise, thanks for hearing me out. Nothing ventured, nothing lost.

A small addendum—there is a lot more to tell, but I am being purposely vague. I will know immediately if you are faking the funk, so don't even try. I may not have sniffed you out before, but I am now a *bona fide* member of "The Dreamseers Club." And we are discerners.

Forever, the Dreamer

Samara closed her laptop and returned it to the desk. Suddenly, she didn't feel so alone. Writing the blog had been surprisingly therapeutic. The good reverend just might be onto something. Journaling was a good way to hear what she was thinking.

She plugged her phone into the charger and sent a quick text to her children letting them know she was okay and that she loved them dearly. She would call Matthew in the morning and invite him over for a home-cooked meal. It would be her way of thanking him for everything. If she had learned anything from her beloved nana, it was how to pray and cook. It would take both of those virtues to whip up the kind of meal that would have made her proud.

She rooted through her CD collection. It was time to turn the music back on. On the other hand, maybe she would listen to her grandmother's audio Bible collection. The guy from Best Buy had done an awesome job hooking up the new Bose system. Incredibly tiny speakers with an amazingly big sound were strategically located throughout the house. One remote control was all that was needed to operate her stereo from any room.

Yep. Crying time was over. Samara popped a Bible CD in the disc player and switched off the light. Better get some sleep. Registration for the next semester at the Bible College was early that next morning. Noah had suggested she take some courses since she had decided to follow this thing through. Souls were at stake, and nobody was going down on her watch. If she was going to do this, then she would do it right—just like her nana would want her to. She would start with getting to know the One who had given her the dreams in the first place.

She nestled under warm blankets, feeling safe and secure. If the little demon was coming for her again, she would be ready. The last thing she remembered hearing before drifting off to sleep was, "In the beginning was the word …"

* * *

"Well done, Lariel." Michael commended the guardian. "The Highest has expressed complete satisfaction with the progress that has been made. Your subject has learned well. You should expect to receive further direction regarding the next phase of her assignment. She is ready."

"In His service, my prince. I will remain with the human until I hear from you otherwise."

"Excellent." Michael prepared to leave. "For Him who sits on the throne, and for the Lamb!"

"Glory and honor to Him who sits on the throne, and to the Lamb!" Lariel saluted.

A cautious smile settled over his face as the prince departed. The human had arrived at her predetermined place of purpose. She was learning to accept that which the Highest had already determined would be. This was critical to the mission because she could not move forward without full acquiescence. They had been waiting for the turning point, and this was it.

All was quiet for now. Lariel planned to make the best of it. A flash of radiant light exploded in the hallway outside of Samara's room as the gigantic wings blended into his form. He winked at the faithful dog lying at the top of the stairway. Max returned the favor by wagging his tail.

Lariel proceeded to check on the rest of the house, beginning with the always-hungry human in the kitchen. No telling how long the calm would last. Mastema had most likely sent out his best reconnaissance task force. The guardian would be waiting for them.

Made in the USA
Lexington, KY
05 September 2014